THE
BUTCHER
AND THE
WREN

THE
BUTCHER
AND THE
WREN

ALAINA URQUHART

zando
NEW YORK

The characters and events in this book are fictitious.
Any similarity to real persons, living or dead,
is coincidental and not intended by the author.

Zando
zandoprojects.com

First Edition: September 2022

Text design by Pauline Neuwirth, Neuwirth & Associates
Cover design by Evan Gaffney

The publisher does not have control over and is not responsible for
author or other third-party websites (or their content).

Library of Congress Control Number: 2022935052

ISBN 978-1-63893-014-3 (Hardcover)
ISBN 978-1-63893-076-1 (B&N)
ISBN 978-1-63893-015-0 (Ebook)

10 9 8 7 6 5 4 3
Manufactured in the United States of America

For Mom and Dad, who are not required to read this book.
You certainly didn't inspire the events (can you imagine?),
but you inspired the act of writing. You got a weird kid, and
you somehow knew what to do. Forever in awe of that.

For John, who gives me the confidence to create.
I adore you more with each passing year.
Never stop singing nineties R&B ballads
at inopportune times.

For my three wonderful babies, who write better books
and have better hair than I ever will.
You can't read this book. Put it down now.

THE
BUTCHER
AND THE
WREN

PART

ONE

CHAPTER 1

JEREMY HEARS THE SCREAMING THROUGH the vents. Hears it but doesn't react. His nighttime routine is essential. The mundane, everyday tasks that he engages in make him more himself. The simple act of wrenching on the ancient faucet on his tidy bathroom vanity grounds and centers him. His night usually ends standing in front of this mirror. He is freshly showered, and, normally, he follows it with a close, leisurely shave. He likes to crawl into bed with a clean body and mind. He takes the time to ensure these preparations happen nightly, regardless of any outside disruption.

Tonight, a particularly loud screech pulls him from his routine. He stares into the mirror, feeling rage entangle itself into his senses. He can feel it rising like an invasive rot. He can't think with the almost rhythmic screaming now rising from the basement. For as long as he can remember, he has hated loud noises. As a child he would feel his surroundings close in on him like a vise whenever he was amid the sounds of a crowded place. Now, the only noises he craves are those of the bayou. Its symphony of creatures soothes him like a warm blanket. Nature always makes the best soundtrack.

He tries to block out the screaming. This routine is sacred. He sighs, pushing a piece of blond hair that has fallen lightly against his forehead back into place and flicking on the radio next to the sink. The only other time he can find solace in sound is when he listens to music. As he prepares for relief, "Hotline Bling" by Drake blares through the speakers, and he flicks it off immediately. Sometimes he feels like he was born in the wrong generation.

He slowly washes away the blood and grime from his hands, trying not to concern himself with the muffled, agonized moans that loudly escape through the heating vents. He looks hard at his face in the mirror. Each year, he feels as though his cheekbones have risen slightly and become more prominent. It is an oddly satisfying consequence that aging has thrust upon him, and he feels blessed for it. A lot of well-adjusted people admire a well-sculpted skull. Most of them don't even understand how primitively ominous that particular fixation is. Most people don't allow themselves to see the savage side of a psyche that was crafted millions of years ago out of their ancestors' often brutal need to survive. These are the traits that evolution deemed to be useful. People are just too dumb to understand that their own predilections are suggestive of a gene pool that is rooted in brutality.

He doesn't necessarily look like someone entangled in depravity. He appears innocuous, and, at times, could look downright wholesome. That's why it all works. There is a plant called *Amorphophallus titanum* that is colloquially re-ferred to as the corpse flower. It's large, beautiful, and without any outward mechanism that would suggest it is dangerous. Yet, when it blooms, every ten years or so, it releases an odor that resembles rotting flesh. It survives though. It thrives. He is not so different from the corpse flower. People flock to this curious plant, and it has cultivated a base of admiration de-spite its quirks.

Tomorrow is Thursday. Thursdays are his Friday, but he truly hates when people say things like that. Regardless, he has enjoyed the luxury of taking Fridays off work since he started his second year at Tulane University School of Medicine. Even though he has some classes to slog through, Fridays are the beginning of his weekend. His weekends are when he gets the most work done. He is particularly excited because he has real plans for his current houseguests this upcoming weekend. Of course, executing those plans to their full potential relies on his ability to add one more to their group.

Emily would indeed be joining them. It had been weeks of analysis after first initiating their partnership in Biology lab, and he is now sure that she would bring the challenge he is craving. Emily jogs a few times a week and doesn't seem to fill her body with trash, so she likely has stamina. She lives with two roommates in Ponchatoula, where they rent a large old home together off campus. Aside from her willingness to reveal too much about herself to her new lab partner, she is competent, self-reliant, and intelligent, all of which would serve her well during his game. Her cohorts would also bring their own value, but he imagines after their extended stay at his home, they won't be up for the entire weekend of activities that he has planned for them.

His other two guests endured a bit of poking and prodding since they arrived the previous Saturday night. At Buchanan's, he managed to engage with them without any prior preparation. Usually, he took time to get to know his potential guests as he did with Emily, but these two fell into his hands. It's like the universe was asking him to take out its trash. Of course, he obliged.

Katie and Matt are painfully generic. They lack any sense of unique thought and were all too eager to follow some good bone structure home with merely the promise of drugs. Katie and Matt know now that they made a poor choice. Again, he hears an anguished moan escape the heating vent, and finds himself losing patience.

He abandons his bedtime ritual and hurries down the stairs to the basement where his guests are staying. He can immediately hear Katie's low moans turn to fearful yelps, and her petite frame physically recoils as he approaches her.

"You need to be cognizant of the fact that you are staying in someone else's home," he says, looking her straight in her muddy brown eyes.

She is hopelessly unremarkable. Brown, lifeless hair sticks to her neck with old blood like crude glue. Her aesthetic is entirely trailer park, though she's desperately tried to hide it. The slightly mouselike aspect to her teeth could be considered charming if she wasn't such an unimaginable twit. When he approached her in the bar, she was regaling Matt with an anecdote about her high school cheerleading days—a pathetic tale that seemed far-fetched considering the shape she is in now. He adjusts the ligatures that hold her to her chair and checks that the IV bag is properly hydrating her system. No kinks in the line, and the bag is still almost full.

"Matt is being respectful. Be more like Matt, Katie." He smiles wide and gestures to Matt's silent and motionless body slumped in the chair beside her.

They both know he passed out, likely from shock, during Jeremy's previous visit down here. Katie begins to weep loudly, and he rolls his eyes. She is testing his gentility, and he is becoming significantly more disgusted by her desperation. He stands quietly in the dark by her side, pressing play on the portable speaker between the two chairs. "A Girl Like You" by Edwyn Collins fills the space. He grins to himself. Finally, a decent sound.

"Ah, that's more like it." He sways to the music, and he gives Katie the opportunity to collect herself.

By the end of the first chorus, she starts wailing. Without hesitation, he grabs the pliers behind her chair, and with one swift motion rips the putridly pink nail clean off her left thumb. He pulls her screaming face to touch his own.

"Another sound out of you, and I start pulling out teeth. Understood?" he threatens.

All she manages is a nod, and he tosses the pliers in the corner. With a wink, he makes his way upstairs.

He didn't grow up with a lot of mercy. He didn't grow up with a lot of anything at all. His father was a tough man but a fair one, expecting a certain level of submission in his home from both wife and son. If Jeremy caught him at just the right time, he learned lasting skills and lessons through his father's careful instruction. As an aircraft machinist in the city, Jeremy's father maintained various pieces of aerospace equipment. Although it didn't require formal education, Jeremy was always proud that his father worked with planes and eager for a glimpse into one of mankind's most significant inventions. But at the wrong time, he was met instead with cruel degradation.

Despite his father's volatility, Jeremy looked forward to his arrival home from work every day. They didn't do much together, but that's what he appreciated. After spending all day with his mother, he would relish the comfortable silence hanging between them as they watched something on television before bed. His days were mostly filled with a heavy dose of neglect sprinkled with some overly attentive moments from his mother, as if she couldn't regulate her affection. She was always far too much or far too little.

A steady respite from the unpredictable whims of his parents, books always held Jeremy's focus. By age seven, he hadn't entered school yet. As neglectful as she could be, every few days, his mother would bring him to a library off St. Charles Avenue. They always went on weekdays, while his father was working. Jeremy didn't understand at the time that his mother was dragging her only child to a library so she could carry on an affair with one of the librarians, but he did absorb the lessons in deception that these trips afforded. He learned early on to never tell his father that his mother left him alone to wander the stacks while she retreated to a back room with Mr. Carraway. More importantly, he taught himself to steal.

He brought home books in his coat or backpack, never relying on his mother to check them out. Jeremy is fairly certain now that the employees had simply looked the other way out of pity, but at the time he felt like he was pulling off a weekly heist.

Now and then, Miss Knox, one of the librarians, would attempt conversation with him. One day, daring to ask directly if everything was okay at home, her voice trembled with concern. He hadn't responded and instead asked her for a book about lobotomies. He had recently become entranced with this archaic medical procedure and its most ardent practitioner, Dr. Walter Freeman. Over the weekend, his father had been watching a rerun episode of *Frontline* called "Broken Minds." It was a brutal look into the mental health system and highlighted a method of lobotomizing patients diagnosed with any number of ailments, especially schizophrenia, by severing the presumed circuit or network of circuits that they believed to be responsible for the patient's atypical behavior.

Dr. Freeman's prefrontal lobotomy captivated him the most. The nickname "ice pick lobotomy" was an exceptionally provocative moniker. It conjured up images of an immaculate surgeon, twisted with the desire to explore the mentally ill mind. Later in 1992, when he heard the term carelessly tossed around in the news as a method serial killer Jeffrey Dahmer was using to subdue his victims, he was disgusted. Dahmer was so feebleminded that he thought he could make his own zombies by injecting cleaning products and acids into his victim's brains. He was imbecilic. To call what he was doing a "lobotomy" is like calling what Ted Bundy was doing "dating." Jeremy could practically hear Dr. Freeman rolling over in his grave.

Jeremy was a kid who craved knowledge. And chronically understimulated, he fed his own hunger by experimentation. His father's early advice echoed in his mind over the years.

"You want to learn about something, son? You have to open it up."

CHAPTER 2

THE LOUISIANA AIR FEELS IMPENETRABLE, even at this early hour. Forensic pathologist Dr. Wren Muller is still blinking the sleep from her eyes as she steps out of her car and into the muggy night. She checks her watch and cringes, thinking how great it would be if criminals could take their nefarious dealings out of the two a.m. hour for a couple of months at least.

She steps over some thick, soggy vegetation, steadying herself on the exposed roots of a nearby bald cypress tree. The grooves of the trunk feel as if they could swallow her up, like the crumbling hands of some ancient, folkloric bayou creature. She stops, waiting for her eyes to adjust to the artificial light ahead. The flashlights of three police officers point downward at something on the banks of the water. Their beams of light cut through the darkness, casting everything around them in an even thicker layer of black. The contrast is welcome. It helps the scene come into better focus.

The dead woman's seminude body is crumpled beneath a substantial amount of tall grass that lines the water's edge. Her head and shoulders are completely submerged in the murky black water. The rest of her body is lying faceup, curled in the grass. The woman is tall and of average weight. As Wren glances over her shoulder, she can see the deputy coroners trailing behind with a stretcher between them. Even between the three of them, it will still be a struggle to get her out of this foreboding bayou.

Only two weeks earlier, investigators recovered the decomposing body of another young woman from behind Twelve Mile Limit bar. She was found facedown in a puddle and drenched with foul-smelling swamp water. The parallels are not lost on Wren as she surveys the area, and although the alarm bells start ringing right away, she tempers them. She always receives a body without bias or expectation. But even while she maintains a single-minded focus on this unique Jane Doe, she makes a mental note to check for hidden items left by the killer. When the previous murder victim was found two weeks ago, they found several crumpled pages from a book shoved halfway down her throat. They were waterlogged and mostly illegible, but one page with the words *Chapter 7* just barely visible was mostly intact.

She carefully creeps closer to the present situation. Jane Doe is missing a shirt, wearing only filthy denim cutoff jeans and a blue bra. There is a large horizontal laceration across her stomach. She has been nearly gutted by something crude. Wren can't help but think of how the cicadas would have been deafening out here. They certainly are right now, as this tired team attempts to piece together this woman's last moments. Was Jane's murderer thinking of the last breaths they stole from her as they dragged her lifeless corpse out here to rot? The thoughts of the depraved fascinated Wren. But the last thoughts of the dead fascinated her even more.

She looks back to the scene and notices a braided bracelet around Jane Doe's left wrist. Its original color was likely crisp white, but now it has taken on the color of something well-worn and well lived. She thinks about the woman buying this innocuous accessory. She can see her picking it up in her hands and turning it over before deciding to buy it. An impulse purchase from an endcap now immortalized in death.

She finds herself closer to the body now. Her coworkers help her pull it onto the sloping shore, slowly slipping the head out of the water to get a better look. The lividity has set noticeably in Jane Doe's face. The coagulated blood that ceased to flow when her heart stopped beating has followed the pull of gravity and crawled across her face, forming blotches that harshly stain her cheeks and forehead. It's difficult to see perfectly with just the dim lights, but Wren thinks that the lividity is a deep pink color, suggesting that the victim took her last breaths about ten hours before this moment. Livor mortis usually begins only about a half hour after death, but you won't see it with any certainty until about two or three hours later. After about six hours, livor mortis darkens into the deep pink color that is obvious to the unaided eye. Bring it to twelve hours after death, and lividity is fixed at its highest level.

When her eyes travel down Jane Doe's face, frozen in an expression of permanent dread, she notices the severe bruising on her neck. There are very clear indications of strangulation. Wren notes these injuries as a reminder to examine them better once she's back in the morgue, and, after slipping on some purple latex gloves, runs a finger over the deep indentations that mar the flesh of the woman's throat.

She pats the outside of Jane Doe's pockets, being careful to feel for anything bulky or sharp. It's incredible how many times she has been thankful for this extra step, feeling a syringe from the outside and avoiding a trip to the clinic. Feeling nothing potentially hazardous, she reaches into Jane's pockets and comes up empty—no identification on the body.

"Anything found around her? A wallet?" Wren asks, though she knows the answer already.

She looks up at the three police officers shining their flashlights down at her for confirmation. All three shake their heads.

The young fellow on the right flippantly moves his flashlight around the area surrounding the body. "What you are seeing, we are seeing. No wallets, no IDs, and no weapon in sight."

While Wren doesn't appreciate the attitude, she nods and manipulates Jane Doe's limbs, revealing an old, faded tattoo on the back of her bicep. It looks like hands set in prayer with a rosary entangled through them.

"Hand me the camera," Wren says, holding out her hand without looking away from the tattoo.

One of her deputy coroners, a new hire, rushes to take it from his bag and nearly fumbles it before placing it in her open hand. Wren snaps a couple of photos of the tattoo before checking for any others.

"We'll get better photos in the autopsy suite, but it is always a good idea to cover your butt and get extra. You never know what can happen in transit. With no ID, we will need all the identifiers we can get, or she will sit in the morgue for months," she explains, handing the camera back to the deputy coroner and cracking her knuckles. She knows it is a terrible habit, but it is her habit, nonetheless. "All right, what can we use to determine the time of death?"

Wren looks up at her two young mentees, and immediately their faces drain of color.

The first stumbles to convey what he obviously knows. "Um, well, there is lividity . . ."

He leans forward and gestures to the red face of Jane Doe.

Wren smirks and nods. "Yes, we see that. How about a less obvious method?"

She knows he is smart. He isn't quick on his feet quite yet, but he knows what needs to be done. Speed will come in time. Soon he won't even think before he acts at a crime scene or back at the office.

He runs a hand through his black hair in a slightly anxious way, and offers, "Rectal temperature?"

Wren gives him a finger gun but then shakes her head with a grimace. "You have good instincts. If we were in a temperature-controlled environment, that would be a great answer. Unfortunately, we can't trust or even wish that the temperature has stayed a balmy eighty-two degrees for this woman's entire time out here." She gestures to the stretcher and instructs, "Open up the bag so we can get her out of here."

As the deputy coroners unfold the white body bag, Wren continues, "You were right with lividity. It is fixed at its highest level, which means we are up at the twelve-hour time frame likely. Grab her arm."

Both attendants move forward, and Wren nods to allow each of them to hold one of Jane Doe's arms.

"Try to manipulate it," she says while she watches them struggle to move it even slightly one way or the other.

"Wow, that's rigid," Wren's mentee points out.

Wren adjusts her gloves farther up her wrist. "Exactly. Rigor is fixed and rigid. It hasn't broken yet. What does this mean?"

The police officers on the scene are clearly annoyed. They make a point to sigh and look dramatically up at the sky as if they have anything else to be doing in the middle of the night. Their display of impatience doesn't shake her. If she has to be awake and in a swamp with a dead woman at three a.m., she will at least train some rookies in the process.

The deputy coroner nearest her stands, smoothing out his pants, "Well, it fits with the twelve-hour time frame. Could be even longer, upwards of thirty hours with this type of rigidity."

There he is.

His growing confidence is promising. With a caseload like hers, Wren can use all the competent help she can find.

"Bingo. And look what we have here," she says and points to the spree of black flies that everyone keeps swatting out of their faces. "I know there are myriad bugs around here, but this little guy is a blowfly. They arrive first to a corpse, and lay eggs that hatch into maggots. We don't have maggots quite yet, but eggs could have been laid at this point. This all still puts us within our estimated range. It looks like the killer could have even done this in the middle of the day. Whoever did this is a brazen bastard."

The rookies are playing the part of captivated students, but the way they both lean on one leg then the other, slightly swaying to keep themselves awake, tells Wren she has lost her audience. Before they turn to leave, a young police officer calls to them from along the tree line.

He is holding a flashlight and pointing it down, exclaiming, "Hey! I got some clothing over here!"

Wren can't contain the snicker that escapes her lips, as she snidely remarks, "And to think, you were ready to clear the scene."

The officer from earlier shoots her an indignant look before walking toward the trees. Wren follows, motioning for the techs to hang back with the body. As they approach the area illuminated by the flashlight, a couple of out-of-place objects come into focus. There nestled under a bush is a filthy yellow T-shirt folded neatly, with a pair of black flip-flops on top. A photo is taken before an officer picks each item up and drops it into an evidence bag. As the shirt unfolds, something drops to the ground with a small thump.

"Is that a book?" Wren questions as she squats down and clicks on her own small flashlight.

In front of her is a small paperback titled *The Ghouls*. Closer inspection reveals it to be an anthology of horror tales. Someone behind snaps another photo, and Wren lifts the book as she stands up. She turns it over in her hands and holds it out to the officers in front of her.

"Ever heard of this title?"

They all shake their heads. One of them holds out a gloved hand to take it.

"Do you think it's Doe's?" he wonders, opening the pages absentmindedly.

"Guess we will find out," Wren retorts, watching him place it into a bag with the clothing for processing.

She turns on her heel, sinking into the moist ground beneath her. It's with an audible squelch that she frees her foot enough to make her way back to the stretcher. She helps them get Jane Doe into the bag and onto the gurney, taking note of the color of the lividity again before removing her gloves. In different light, it appears an even brighter shade of pink. She walks back to the coroner van carefully with the body and the two techs trailing behind. Opening the back of the truck, she waits for the crew to struggle their way through the uneven terrain and quietly dreads the idea of another unidentified body in her morgue.

"Who is missing you tonight?" she asks quietly as Jane Doe passes in front of her.

A police officer nearby chuckles.

"A stiff ever answer you back?" he teases.

Wren looks him in the eyes before slamming the door shut and walking to the driver's-side door.

"You'd be surprised how many secrets the dead have told me."

CHAPTER 3

MORNINGS ARE NICE. JEREMY CRAVES a strong cup of coffee, and he always makes sure to eat breakfast. The remainder of the day is often scattered and unpredictable, with his lunch breaks spent doing research, so he cannot always make time for full meals. He glances up at the small television on the kitchen counter. The news is in its second week of covering the story of two escaped convicts from Clinton Correctional Facility in Dannemora, New York. Even in Louisiana, people are captivated by the tale of a lovestruck prison worker helping two convicted murderers escape like a real-life *Shawshank Redemption*.

While watching, he scrambles some eggs and eats them with turkey sausage. He has considered becoming vegetarian for the health benefits but fails to rationalize it properly. He does hold animals at a higher level of respect than he does most members of his own species, but mostly due to their ability to survive as soon as they enter the world. Empathy doesn't enter the equation, which is why he doesn't feel the need to deprive himself of an easy source of protein. After cleaning his plate, he makes his way downstairs to check on his guests.

Katie is noticeably quiet.

"She must value those mouse teeth," he muses to himself.

Her left hand is caked in blood that has dripped and dried around the leg of her chair and the floor below. She's slumped into a self-soothing position, which makes him feel an intense desire to disrupt her. Unfortunately, he is running late and doesn't have time for extraneous pleasure this morning. Instead, he gives her a wink. Upon seeing him, Matt begins to throw a testosterone-fueled tantrum, spitting and cursing at him while trying to tear his arms free of the chains that bind him. He can see that Matt spent his night trying to dislodge the chair from the basement floor, but all he's managed to do is splinter some of its leg. These chairs were cemented into the foundation long ago. They're not going anywhere. As a matter of due diligence, he thinks for a moment about what Matt's plan would be should he miraculously topple the chair over, but he quickly decides not to waste his time. Matt is too stupid and increasingly too weak to best him. He checks on their IV bags and starts to replenish them while Matt does his best tough-guy impression.

"I swear I will fucking rip you apart, you pussy!" he screams, spraying foul spit onto Jeremy's cheek.

He thinks about taking some pliers to Matt's front teeth but doesn't have another clean ironed dress shirt to change into now. Besides, it is hard to feel anything but disgust for a man sitting in his own piss and still using words like *pussy*. He responds instead by aggressively grabbing Matt's face and planting a deep kiss right on his mouth, biting hard enough on his bottom lip to hear a satisfying crunch. Sometimes he allows himself to give in to hedonistic instincts, and rarely does he regret it.

"You came here willingly. Remember that," he growls as Matt's mouth fills with blood.

Matt sputters and yells incoherently while Katie quietly whimpers beside him. Jeremy smiles in return as he heads upstairs, using a tissue to wipe away Matt's blood from his mouth and giving himself a quick once-over in the hallway mirror. He pushes a stray blond hair back into place and walks out the door.

His day job is data entry and billing for a warehousing and logistics company. It is exactly as dull and mindless as it sounds, and he loathes that he has to spend the bulk of his week regurgitating numbers into a computer program. Today he walks into the lobby of Lovett Logistics after leaving the thick atmosphere outside. Summertime in Louisiana makes walking across a parking lot feel like trudging through warm butter. Heavy, humid, and oppressive. Inside, he feels his body struggle to acclimate to the canned cold air that pumps out of every direction. Between the overused air-conditioning, the slack-jawed company men, and the knowledge that he'll be crammed into this petri dish for the next few hours, it is an absolute waking nightmare for him. He reaches into his bag and realizes that he forgot the ID card that grants him access into the building, thanks to Katie's distractions last night. With a quiet sigh, he approaches the woman behind the front desk. She is slightly overweight, with arms that remind him of oiled, crispy chicken skin that she routinely shows off with sleeveless dresses and blouses. Her round face is framed with overprocessed blond hair that clearly doesn't grow from her dark roots. He has never bothered to see what color her eyes are, because the amount of makeup she applies to them makes him sick to his stomach. Today, he spots shades of green, like a fungus has taken up residence in her ocular cavities, breaking through her eyelids to colonize the rest of her plump face. As usual, she is swiping away on her phone, no doubt checking on the masses of heathens who fill her inbox with vaguely assaulting propositions on whatever dating app she hopes will bring her to her soul mate.

"Can I do something for you, Jeremy?" she asks as he approaches.

He winces when she uses his name, as he has made it a point to deny committing hers to memory. He plasters on a friendly smile and leans his elbow on the desk in front of her.

"You can be an angel and override the door lock for me," he charms, gesturing to his bag, "I forgot my key card, and am just itching to get in there and get to work."

She laughs loudly, covering her mouth as if it will make her look like a lady. He resists the urge to heave, and instead chuckles along with her. She smiles and presses the override key with an acrylic nail.

"You owe me," she says with a wink.

"I don't owe you shit," he responds to her coldly as he leaves the lobby. She will probably take his comment as a joke. He doesn't care either way.

CHAPTER 4

WREN SECURES HER FACE SHIELD and silently gazes over the body that lays before her on the cold morgue gurney. The woman looks back at her from behind one saggy eyelid. Even the sliver of her right eye screams of the horrors she endured.

Her waterlogged clothing has already been photographed and removed. Technicians are now scanning them for a fiber, hair, or anything that could be traced back to the beast that did this. Wren palpates for signs of broken bones, taking special note of the petechial hemorrhage still visible on her face even though decomposition has already started to ravage her features. The Louisiana sun is pretty unforgiving to the living, but it is particularly cruel to the dead. Wren estimates that this victim was outside in the elements for maybe a day, as evidenced by the slight bloat and lack of significant putrefaction.

She notes the bruising around her throat, where multiple ligatures intersected and cut deeply into the tissue surrounding the larynx. This wasn't the cause of death. Besides the stomach wound that Wren is betting was the fatal blow, the bruising on her neck indicates blood flow, which only occurs when a heart is beating. This poor girl was mechanically strangled without the intent of death. Her brutal strangulation was just something her killer enjoyed before finally giving her the release of death, in one of the most painful ways imaginable.

The stomach wound, which runs the length of her abdomen, is jagged and deep. Blood coagulated inside the injury, which indicates that the killer inflicted it while she was still alive. Between the rigor mortis that still lingers in some of her muscles and her liver temperature, time of death hovers somewhere in the past thirty-six hours or so. Unfortunately, the postmortem lividity she determined at the crime scene was slightly less time than that. She'd expect these stains to be deep red, blue, or purple, but the pooled blood under Jane Doe's skin is bright pink.

Wren frowns at the discrepancy but decides to move forward with the examination. Lividity is also helpful in determining whether someone moved the body after death, as was the case with the victim currently on Wren's table. The blood that stopped flowing after the victim's stomach was torn open had pooled on the right side of her hip, face, and small portions of her right arm. The victim was lying on her right side after death. There are also signs of pooling on her lower back and across her shoulders, so she was on her back at one point as well. Given the deeper color lividity on her right side, it is safe to deduce that she died while lying on her right side and was later moved to her back. These details piece together like a neatly fitted puzzle, but the color of the lividity still gives Wren pause.

Detective John Leroux enters the room, snapping a mask around his face and slipping his right hand into a latex glove. His angular jaw is set into a noticeable clench, and his deeply blue eyes, the only thing visible above the mask, seem to ask a million questions.

Wren looks up briefly as he enters the autopsy suite. She can read his expressions instantly after years of working together. He's overworked and hoping for answers.

"Tell me you have something to give me here, Muller," he says as he adjusts his waistband, placing his hands on his hips.

Wren hesitates a moment before looking up.

"He refrigerated her."

CHAPTER 5

Taking a seat in his cubicle, Jeremy flicks on his computer screen and arranges his coffee and cell phone within reach. He prefers to ease himself into the day with a couple of passes through news sites and social media. Today, the front page of the *Times-Picayune* website catches his eye. "Search for Missing Orleans Parish Man and Woman Intensifies as Friends Continue to Hold Vigil." He can hardly stifle his laughter. Vigils always fascinated him.

What good are your candles and photographs doing while Katie and Matt suffer in my basement?

He infers that these "friends" in the article photos, teary-eyed and solemn, are more interested in seeing themselves in print. Everyone has a motive. It is clear from their willingness to boast about their loss that these folks are basking in the spotlight to satisfy their own disgusting need for attention. He scans the rest of the article, which details the immediate need to locate these two blights on the gene pool.

"Scary as hell, right?" his coworker Corey interrupts, leaning his elbow on the side of Jeremy's cube as he sips his coffee. "These two are going to end up like the rest of them. The similarities are too glaring to ignore, you know? Once he dumps one, he grabs another within days. You heard that they think they found that other girl that was missing, right?" Corey shakes his head and takes another sip of coffee. He is referring to the others, and he is partially correct. Jeremy has been doing this for a while, racking up six victims at this point. Usually, he did precisely what Corey surmised. Once he grew tired of one, he went in search of another. This was the only time he had ever overlapped. Katie and Matt arrived at his home while Meghan was still partially alive. It wasn't the plan, and it was risky, but sometimes improvisation is necessary when the right people show up.

Meghan was a sad, desperate creature whom Jeremy convinced to leave the bar with him last Thursday. She was loud, boisterous, and arrogant, irritating him from the moment she opened her mouth. At one point, she screamed up from the basement, calling him a "mama's boy" and igniting in him a rage that he knew would cloud careful, rational thought. Had he given in to the anger, he may have made a crucial error, and he deeply resented Meghan for almost making him lose his cool, and with it, his freedom.

He spent a few days trying to break her. He tracked her psychological state as she wondered what day, what hour, and what minute would be her last. And after a few days of playing, he walked down to the basement in silence. His sudden lack of interaction should have been an omen, but she still didn't see it coming when he plunged a knife directly into her stomach. He dragged it across her abdomen with great force and watched as she writhed in pain on the concrete basement floor. He chose this end deliberately. Stomach wounds are truly harrowing. Bile and acid pour into the wound, slowly poisoning the victim with their own bodily fluids.

That was Sunday night, one day after Katie and Matt arrived. Meghan's body had been found this morning. He heard about it briefly on the radio, but they weren't releasing any details to the public yet. He isn't nervous. He always takes great care not to leave a trace anywhere on the body. He had even discarded the lengths of fishing line and electrical cord that he used to strangle Meghan in one of their little games, just to be safe.

Although Jeremy didn't initially set out to have a modus operandi, he usually targeted people in their twenties and thirties outside of bars and nightclubs. But he always changed up his method of murder, following his curiosities wherever they led. And, of course, there's the swamp water. After victim four turned up, he was given a name by the press due to his penchant for leaving the bodies bathed in filthy swamp water and in plain sight. They called him the Bayou Butcher, which at first he didn't mind but now found tedious. Lately, he has become bored with this stagnant routine. Moreover, if he's becoming predictable, he's edging closer to getting caught. He is ready to serve up a new dish.

Jeremy snaps from his reverie and swivels around in his chair to look up at Corey.

"You think?" Jeremy asks.

Corey chuckles, stretching his hand out to gesture to the part of the article that details the current length of Katie and Matt's disappearance.

"Oh yeah. These two idiots have been missing for almost a full week. They are done. Drench 'em in swamp muck and call it what it is."

Jeremy can't help but grin at Corey's candor. It's refreshing to hear him express as much disdain for Jeremy's houseguests as Jeremy feels for them himself.

"You might be right, man. And hey, at least if they turn up it'll put an end to all those candles and prayers. I can't take much more of these fame whores, desperate for a camera crew's attention," Jeremy offers, testing the limits of Corey's apathy.

Corey belts out a laugh, lurching forward slightly and nodding his head. "You got that right!" he exclaims. "I'm calling it. They'll be worm food by the weekend."

He is almost dead right, which leaves Jeremy a bit disappointed.

"Anyways, I'm getting the eyes, so I better start earning my paycheck," Corey says, rolling his eyes. Jeremy notices their manager peering over at them, basking in the scant amount of power he holds over his cubicle kingdom. Corey knocks the cube wall lightly with his fist, adding, "I almost forgot, I have an open mic spot Saturday night at the Tap. Stop by if you're free. I need all the attendance I can get."

Jeremy nods. "Yeah, man, I will try to stop by. Good luck."

With that, Corey hurries away to his own cube, and Jeremy gets to work.

CHAPTER 6

WREN IS FRUSTRATED. UNIDENTIFIED BODIES in her morgue irritate her endlessly. Mostly, it's due to her own neurotic need to finish what she starts and clear items from her to-do lists. She doesn't like having unfinished business, and especially not when she's reminded of it every time she opens the freezer door. And beyond administrative irritations, these Jane Does bring with them a heavy sadness. She sees them at night when she closes her eyes. She hears them asking her to give them a name, to give them epilogues to their stories. She can't shake the dread that comes with knowing that someone's loved one is lying unclaimed in a cold body bag. The loneliness of the Does haunts her. Nothing is worse than being forgotten. She has made it her mission to never let her Does remain that way for long.

Leroux runs his gloved hand along the pink lividity on the Doe's right arm and looks up at Wren.

"So, he's trying to fuck with your time of death estimate," he states rather than asking.

Wren doesn't take her gaze off the woman.

"Trying . . . succeeding," she replies, shaking her head absentmindedly before turning around to click a new blade onto the scalpel handle.

"That's such a weirdly specific thing to do, ya know? How many of these idiots out there even know you can do that?"

Wren doesn't answer and instead makes a cut to begin the evisceration. She angrily shakes her head. Leroux snickers, stepping back and readjusting the mask on his face.

"I bet it was done with the sole intention of grinding the gears of the county medical examiner," he jokes and tilts his head to the side. "You're giving this guy a lot of credit here. From my experience, they're idiots in wolf's clothing."

Wren stops cutting and gives him an annoyed look.

"I never said it was his sole intention. I just don't like my abilities being tested by some gutless asshole who thinks he's Hannibal Lecter or something."

She pulls out a tool like a pair of hedge clippers and begins using it to snap each rib from the bottom up to the clavicle. The force and sound of snapping ribs make for perfect catharsis whenever she feels frustrated. The dense clavicle bone takes some extra elbow grease to crack, a job she relishes at this moment.

"Well then, you will hate this next piece of information." Leroux steps to the side, allowing her to get to the left side of the rib cage.

She groans without pausing her work.

"Spit it out," she hisses between the sharp sound of snapping bone.

He silences the call coming through on his cell phone and leans on the counter, "We are pretty positive we have a serial killer on our hands."

"No?!" she says with fake incredulity.

He stays silent but gives her a stony look in response.

"I could have told you that, John. When do I get my detective badge?" Wren retorts and rolls her eyes, allowing a smirk.

He closes his eyes in exasperation. "All right, well that's not the real kicker here, Muller." He walks around the other side of the table and leans forward on his hands. "This potential serial killer is leaving clues about his next body drops. We think we may have a lead on another scene, but we can't decipher it yet."

"You're going to have to elaborate for me, pal." Wren turns to face him and cocks her head to the side.

"Stand down, Muller. We aren't one hundred percent yet. The next drop's location may be what he is trying to tell us with the garbage he left on the bodies. That victim found behind Twelve Mile Limit? I am sure you remember the paper shoved down her throat."

Wren stops what she is doing and nods, urging him to continue. There were two recent bodies found with strange items at the scenes. She can't help but sneer at the idea of a killer trying to be theatrical. Is it not enough drama to take a life away? Are they so starved for validation that they have to package their carnage up like a Jack in the Box toy? It's always about control. This kind of monster feels power in making sure everyone knows that he is in charge. Wren knows though that these calling cards indicate insecurity more than confidence, like someone who tells a joke but then spends a half hour explaining the punch line. They don't let it speak for itself. It's desperate and uncomfortable behavior. It is a move used by only the most pathetic big-name killers, obsessively narcissistic little demons who demand a standing ovation.

Dennis Rader, aka BTK, didn't stop at stalking, brutalizing, and murdering innocent women in their homes in the 1970s. He was so impatient for infamy that he called the police to direct them to his crime scenes. When he grew tired of merely reporting his own deeds, he took to writing letters and poems to the press and leaving strange little murder dioramas around town for law enforcement. His thirst for attention was his undoing in the end. He got so sloppy in his haste to be the next big thing that he genuinely asked law enforcement in a letter if they could trace a floppy disk back to him. They said they could not, and he believed them. He thought himself so powerful and untouchable that even police would bend to his vaudevillian aspirations. He was wrong.

"The lab was able to see what was on it, at least partially. It was the seventh chapter of a dime novel. Pop quiz, in what swamp did we find our second scene?"

"Seven Sisters Swamp," she says contemplatively. "Isn't that kind of a tenuous connection though? I agree, it's strange but . . ."

Leroux puts up a finger to stop her before she can finish her thought. "The book found at the Seven Sisters Swamp crime scene had one chapter torn out of it. Chapter seven. And we confirmed it is from the same book."

He looks pleased with himself, before gesturing to what used to be a living human being.

"And that's not all. A piece of scrap paper was tucked into her clothing. We're looking into it for any indication of the next scene. I've got all my people on it but made a photocopy for you too. It would help to have another set of eyes on it."

He takes a paper out of his back pocket and unfolds it before placing it on the counter in front of Wren. She pulls the glove off her hand and inspects the copy.

"This fleur-de-lis pattern . . ." Wren leans over the gurney that holds the victim's body and points at the pattern that borders part of the scrap paper. "Is it matte, or did it have a sheen to it?"

"It was kind of shiny. What's that word?" He squeezes his eyes shut and holds up a fist, then points a finger. "Iridescent. Kind of embossed too."

She nods and continues studying the photocopy. "What is this other thing on here?"

He leans forward slightly as she tips the paper toward his eyeline.

"Ah, that's a copy of the library card from the book. Again, more eyes on it are always helpful."

"Philip Trudeau. That name feels so familiar," Wren muses, staring at the last name written on the library card.

"Well, unfortunately, it turned out to be a dead end." Leroux groans and waves his hand.

"Yeah, I'm no murder police, but my civilian intuition tells me that when a perp writes down their name and number at the scene of the crime, it's probably too good to be true."

"Yeah, yeah. We got a hold of this Philip Trudeau. Lives up in Massachusetts. Guy hasn't been to Louisiana since he was in middle school, some twenty-odd years ago. And this book was accounted for at Lafayette Public Library up until about ten days ago," Leroux explains. He rechecks his phone and sighs. "I gotta take this, but keep thinking on it."

He hurries out the morgue door. Wren places the photocopy on the counter behind her and pulls a clean glove onto her hand. She lifts the chest plate out of the victim's body and looks at the clock above the door.

"It's going to be a long night, hun."

CHAPTER 7

CLOCKING OUT OF WORK AT 5:08 p.m., Jeremy gathers his things and makes his way toward the door.

"Saturday!" Corey yells from across the sea of cubicles.

Jeremy raises a hand in acknowledgment but silently breezes past the front desk and into the parking lot. He lets out a heavy sigh and feels the stress release from his body almost immediately. Life in a cubicle is truly barbaric.

As he sits down in his car, the weight of a day's worth of sun presses upon him. Turning on the air conditioner doesn't provide any immediate relief. Instead, he is assaulted by hot, stale air from all sides. Opening the window only slightly lessens the feeling of suffocation. As he regulates his stifled breathing in response to the burst of cool air at last pumping through the vents, Jeremy can't help but wonder if this is how it feels to be strangled to death; a brief moment of helpless, nauseating panic followed by a sudden sense of relief.

But Jeremy isn't interested in the business of granting relief. No, he is focused solely on inflicting pain. The mechanics of pain are both intricate and simple, a fundamental dichotomy. Physiologically, pain requires a perfect symphony of chemical reactions. Each piece hitting at just the correct time for the feeling to materialize. A stimulus sends an impulse across a peripheral nerve fiber, which is in turn perceived and identified by the somatosensory cortex. If any part of the stimulus's journey is interrupted, then the feeling will be diminished. In contrast, the act of sending that electrical impulse on its journey to perception is something even troglodytes could master. All it takes is an object, sharp or blunt, coupled with force. What a fascinating thing.

He remembers the first time he saw pain and recognized it. He must have been seven years old, reading a book in the living room of the home he still lives in today. As he turned the page, he heard it. Outside, he listened to his father's truck pull into the dirt driveway. The door opened and then slammed shut with a force that suggested he was keyed up. He could hear him grumbling to himself out there, cursing and spitting as he shuffled to his shed.

Jeremy jumped up and ran outside to see what was going on and when he did, he heard something new. The sound came from the bed of the pickup truck in front of him, and it was agonizing. At first, he swore there was an injured child in the back of that truck. The cry was so human and so tortured—a series of wails followed by low, painful moans. It fascinated and repelled him in equal measure, and he felt every cell in his body vibrating with anticipation. The heat of that late afternoon beat down on him like a weighted blanket, ominous and foreboding, and warning him to seek sanctuary. But still, he was compelled, as if being pulled by an invisible string, toward the screaming form in the bed of the truck. Hoisting himself up to see inside, he saw lying twisted in front of him a terrified doe. He noted her clearly broken leg and an open wound that extended from the left corner of her mouth down to her shoulder. Her sides and stomach rose and fell with such labored, excruciating breaths that air seeped from his own lungs in response. Blood dripped from her nose, and her eyes were wild with fear and pain. He could still see those eyes today when he closed his own. He couldn't look away. For a few seconds, he just stood there, sharing a nightmarish moment with a beautiful creature.

As if on cue, music began to cut through the air. His father had switched on the ancient radio in his shed. He always liked to have music playing while working. "These Boots Are Made for Walkin'" by Nancy Sinatra slithered from the speakers.

"Son, get down from there. You're gonna scare it, and I need that goddamn screaming to stop," his father instructed as he strolled back from the shed in the side yard.

He had a hunting rifle slung over his shoulder, and he gestured his hand to wave Jeremy away from the screaming animal before him.

"Dad, what happened?" Jeremy asked tentatively, jumping down from his vantage point.

His father ran a hand through his sandy hair and then rubbed his chin anxiously. It made a familiar scratching sound.

"She ran out too quickly in front of the truck. The damn thing was so twisted up, lying in the road. I couldn't leave it screaming there. I didn't have a gun with me, so here we are," he responded matter-of-factly as he walked around to the back of the truck and pulled the tailgate down.

Jeremy could see her better now, lying on an old dirty drop cloth that was once white but had since turned a foul shade of beige from use. Stains of blood bloomed on the fabric. Now the doe's tongue was protruding out of her mouth. As he stared, his father wheeled a large wheelbarrow over to the tailgate and looked at Jeremy.

"Good thing I got you here, boy," he said slapping Jeremy on the back and making him lurch forward.

"What are you going to do?" he asked earnestly.

"Well, we have to kill it. We would be monsters to let it suffer for too long."

Jeremy felt his breath hitch in his throat.

"Kill it?" he asked, never breaking his gaze from the doe's.

"It's life, son. You don't let something suffer needlessly. And besides, there's a pecking order. Some are on the top, and some are here to provide something to those on the top. This doe's sacrifice will provide good meat," he explained and yanked on the drop cloth, causing the injured animal to shudder with the sudden movement. "Come on, help me pull her down."

Jeremy was awestruck. He robotically helped his father pull the drop cloth toward the tailgate and climbed into the bed with the doe to lower her down while his father pulled. Now the noises were loud and urgent. She was calling out, trying to alert her kin for help, but she was too far from home now.

She hit the wheelbarrow with a repulsive thud. A slight cracking sound and more high-pitched screams followed. His father quickly wheeled the creature to the back of the house, and Jeremy followed wordlessly. When they had reached the tree line, he helped dump the doe onto the grass.

"Come next to me, son," his father beckoned him away from the creature and to his side.

He lined up his shot, standing with his foot touching the doe's back leg and the rifle angle down and toward her head. The doe screamed louder, like she could sense the doom standing next to her.

"Now, you want to hit it between the eyes," he said quietly. "Dispatching an injured animal should be quick."

With that last word, he squeezed the trigger without warning. Jeremy's body jumped with the sudden sound. Everything seemed like it slowed down for a second as the doe's head snapped back with the impact. Then the silence crashed down like heavy rain, causing him to shiver with its arrival. They stood together for a moment, his father and him. Looking back, Jeremy considers that day vital in his development. He saw suffering, pain, and the release of death.

Jeremy walks through his home's front door and tosses his keys into a copper dish just inside. He imagines that the sudden sound of metal hitting metal probably startles his guests, and the thought of their fear excites him. He walks straight to the sink in the kitchen and begins to scrub his hands vigorously, ridding them of the germs he no doubt picked up at the office. Unbuttoning his dress shirt, he excitedly makes his way toward the basement door. He only stops briefly to hang his shirt on a hook placed strategically on the wall. He smooths his white undershirt before creaking the basement door open and descending the stairs.

CHAPTER 8

WREN SWIPES HER KEY CARD to open the imposing morgue door and makes her way down the steps to the back parking lot. She slides into the driver's seat of her modest black sedan and quickly taps the button to lock the doors. She has seen the aftermath of too many people who sat obliviously in their own vehicles while a predator waited close by.

She sits inside, taking a moment to collect herself before heading home. The hot breeze carries a hushed conversation to the car, and she looks up to find Leroux stalking out of the back door, running a hand through his hair. She's about to call out to him but sees that he's about to be on the phone. She watches him tap his phone's screen and bring it in front of his face. The voice on the other end is on speaker and sounds hurried.

"It's Ben. The book came back clean."

Leroux audibly sighs, ducking behind his own car's steering wheel and slipping a cigarette from the vanity mirror.

"Jesus, not even a partial?"

"I'm sorry, man." Ben sounds genuinely disappointed on the other line. "I thought we might've had something this time."

Leroux holds the cigarette in front of his lips for a moment.

"Did this asshole wear gloves to the library? How does he manage such forensically clean crime scenes?" he vents, lighting up and taking a quick, deep drag. "Man, first Muller gets stumped by this guy, and now you? Where have all my experts gone?"

Wren chafes at this but watches on as he exhales a cloud of smoke that crawls out of his open window. Leroux has been on the job long enough to know that no case wraps itself in a bow like they do on television. But he is used to being able to find a thread to pull somewhere.

Even Israel Keyes, one of the most meticulous and profoundly cunning serial killers the world has ever seen, slipped up eventually. Everything he did was carefully considered. He always traveled, sometimes taking planes and cars and trains, to abduct and kill his random victims, burying kill kits all around the United States so his tools were ready for him when he arrived. After these efforts to distance himself from each of his previous victims, a crime that he committed in his own town led to his capture. When he saw the young barista at the small coffee kiosk in Anchorage that he had planned to rob that evening, he lost years of carefully honed control. He kidnapped, raped, and murdered her in his car without any planning or forethought. His spontaneous abduction was caught on CCTV footage, and when he tried to flee, was captured again by bank cameras after using her debit card on his way out of town. His perfect reign of terror ended with some care-lessness. She hopes this killer will befall a similar fate.

It's all over Detective Leroux's face as he sucks in another cloud of toxins to quiet his jittery nerves. He is wondering if New Orleans has produced a serial killer that defies even Israel Keyes's level of Machiavellian plotting. Ben chuckles from out of the speaker, and a coffee machine can be heard brewing loudly in the background.

"Well, at least Muller is stumped too."

Leroux sighs and answers with a groan, "Looks like it is back to the drawing board. Thanks, man."

"You got it." Ben hangs up his end quickly.

Wren can barely be offended. They've all been working as hard as they can. Leroux really looks like hell. As he flicks his cigarette onto the pavement below and pulls out of the lot, Wren spots the dark circles beneath his eyes. She sighs and turns on her ignition. The sounds of the radio blare through the speakers at an uncomfortable volume that cuts through the silence of the mostly abandoned streets surrounding the morgue. She flicks off the sound and connects her phone to the car's Bluetooth, choosing a podcast for her short drive home. But it brings her no distraction. She can't stop think-ing about the name on the library card. According to Leroux, Philip Trudeau was a red herring, but Wren can't shake the familiar sound of his name.

How many Philip Trudeaus do you meet in a lifetime?

She pulls onto her street and wonders whether she should listen to this nagging sense of dread or if she should trust that Leroux and the other detectives did their due diligence in ruling out the man in Massachusetts. She swings her car into the driveway and walks up the steps to her old rickety porch. Her home definitely wears its age, but she loves its character and many quirks.

Sliding her keys onto the hook by the front door, she walks into her kitchen and drops her bags to the floor. Feeling exhausted but not ready to sleep, she peeks at the stove clock and brews a cup of coffee. Most of her friends take to a hearty chalice of red wine after a long day, but wine never suited Wren. To her, it tastes like chalky grape juice that has been sitting in the sun and only serves to give her a headache. The warm, welcoming smell of freshly brewed coffee puts her mind immediately at ease. She leans against the counter and listens to the spits and gurgles of her drink being made.

Philip Trudeau.

She repeats the name in her mind and then aloud, hoping for a long-forgotten memory to unearth itself spontaneously. She's careful not to wake her husband, Richard, from his slumber upstairs. He works early, and Wren tries to keep her night-owl tendencies from disrupting his rest.

Cradling the coffee mug in her hands, she makes her way to the love seat in the sitting room and plops down onto its well-worn cushions. Richard has been champing at the bit to replace this particular piece with something new, but Wren can't part with it. She likes that it knows her. New furniture always seems to have that lengthy introduction period when it fails to hug you the way you need. The stiffness of a new couch is something she simply doesn't have the patience for, especially lately.

Even as she sips her coffee, she can't just release her day enough even to consider sleep. Her mind keeps wandering back to the victim in her morgue. Her bloated, battered body a speed trap for Wren's thoughts. Her killer is clever—intelligent enough to understand the frustration a previously refrigerated body would cause for someone tasked with determining the time of death. He got smarter with this one too. Took even more care to conceal his identity, which tells Wren that he is capable of learning and adapting. The method by which he takes their lives isn't even consistent, like he is experimenting. He has a curious mind and a researcher's meticulousness, a dangerous combination.

"Wren!"

"What? Hey. Hi, hun," she responds abruptly, shaken from her thoughts by a familiar voice.

Richard yawns and makes his way to the comfortable chair across from her, where he plops down in a heap.

"You with us?" He grins, and she lets out a breathy chuckle.

"Sorry, I didn't want to wake you. I was just trying to wind down a bit before I came to bed."

"Apparently, you wound yourself out of reality for a second there. I said your name twice before you snapped out of it."

"It was a long night."

She leans back and takes a sip of the coffee. He leans forward, putting his hands together and resting his elbows on his knees.

"Yeah, I had a feeling you would be in for the long haul tonight."

He always understands. Sometimes she wonders how, but she never takes his understanding for granted.

"This one is just particularly frustrating, not to mention brutal," she sighs, chewing on her lip. "I just want to find this guy."

"Wren, that's just it. You don't have to find him. That's the detective's job. Just focus on what you do best. Work with the information that is presented to you."

She knows he is right. But he doesn't know about Philip Trudeau and the nagging sensation that there is a connection for her to find. Instead of debating this with him, she humors him and stands up from the love seat.

"You're right, I know."

"Let's go to bed."

Wren nods and makes her way to the sink as Richard shuffles toward the stairs. She dumps the slightly cold coffee left in her mug down the sink drain and catches her own reflection in the window above it. She is a sorry sight tonight.

She notices that her basil plant on the windowsill is on the cusp of wilting. She quickly refreshes it with some water from the faucet, knowing that it will have rejuvenated entirely in a few hours.

"Drink up, little one."

She flicks off the light and makes her way up to the bedroom, wondering if this serial killer ever watered his plants.

CHAPTER 9

THE DRIVE TO SCHOOL CAN take hours in the traffic. Sometimes Jeremy doesn't mind the slow slog. It's a time when he can be completely alone with no one nearby to interrupt his thoughts.

Today is not one of those days.

He's anxious, and his legs have a million tiny insects running around inside of them. He taps and bounces his foot in a fruitless attempt to calm them. It's been a long process of figuring out what he wanted to build for himself next. And now that it's almost here, he can't stop thinking about it. He can't stop seeing his game play out in his head. He feels the environment, and smells the desperation already. Jeremy turns on the radio and pinches the bridge of his nose, flicking the channel to a local station.

"The victim, a white female in her twenties, was found behind a popular local bar early this morning. The body has been transported to the medical examiner and an autopsy is scheduled for later today."

Jeremy can feel his heartbeat quicken and his face flush. There is a particular rush that courses through him whenever he knows this crop of inept detectives has received another of his guests. The only thing stopping them from joining the ranks of the criminals they chase is a kind of false morality. A fragile thing that could shatter at any moment, like blown glass.

And then there's the medical examiner. No matter how deeply MEs believe the dead can speak to them, they can't. They can determine a cause of death—sometimes—but they can't even fathom what went through each victim's mind while sucking in their last gulps of precious, futile air. Forensic pathologists can accurately explain what happens when a heart stops beating. But they can't publish a paper that details what true anguish looks like or catalog the unbridled pleasure that comes from causing it. They've wielded a bone saw but haven't wrapped their hands around someone's neck. Death and pain cannot be explained in an autopsy report, not really. It's primal and cannot be taught in a classroom or lab.

They have no idea what is in store for them, this team of so-called experts, still chasing a systematic killer who has an established pattern. None of them can see a shift in the routine coming. While they scramble to piece together a long-outdated profile, he will be orchestrating his magnum opus.

As the traffic starts to break in front of him, he shakes himself from his reflective daze.

Catch me if you can.

CHAPTER 10

*I*S *THIS DEATH?*

Wren is smothered by a darkness that is so thick she feels like she could chew it. An overwhelming heat consumes her in the dark. Her heart starts to race and the blackness glows red. She wills her mouth open as a trapped sob lies caught in her throat. Her chest aches, and she struggles to yell for help, but nothing comes out.

Then, without warning, the darkness dissolves, and she sees her parents before her. They stand together in a stark-white room, her mother clutching her father's arm. Their faces twist with devastation. She throws her arms around them both at once. She can smell her mother's homey apple scent and her father's safe aroma, clean and warm. She stays glued to them for a moment, letting the relief fill the air.

But it's cold now.

There are no arms embracing her back. She pulls her head back to look up at their faces. When she studies their tear-stained eyes, they just see through her.

"Mom, Dad!" she pleads, placing her hands on their cheeks.

They stay clinging to each other but remain distant from her. She feels hot again. It's a deep, pulsating wave of heat mixed with nausea. She tries again to call for her parents, this time yelling above the white noise now hurting her ears.

"Mom! Where are we? Please help me!" she begs, receiving nothing in return.

Her mother's eyes are worn and red from crying. She looks hopeless and doesn't respond to Wren's wails. Then a sound echoes throughout the static, white environment. It's familiar, but it's neither her parents' voices nor her own.

"You're dying, Wren," a man's voice says casually.

Her blood turns to ice water. She stares into her parents' faces, still clinging to them and not wanting to look behind her. Like smoke, they fade until there is nothing left. She falls forward onto her knees as they disappear in front of her eyes. Another choked sob escapes her, followed by a shiver when he speaks again.

"What's wrong with your legs, Wren?" he asks.

She looks down at the tops of her thighs and stands up from her kneeling position. As she puts her feet on the ground, it's like stepping in water. Her weight shifts, and she wobbles. He's laughing now. A low, cutting sneer escapes from his lips, and as she stumbles back to her knees, he begins to cackle.

"My legs," she whispers.

There isn't any feeling left in them, like dead limbs on an ancient tree. Finally, she turns to look at him as he crosses the space toward her. He's clean, almost sterile, wearing a white T-shirt and jeans without a speck of dirt on them. His face is blurry. As he walks, she feels the air rush out of her lungs. She frantically coughs and gags, feeling like a hot poker has been jammed down her throat.

"Shhhh," he coos softly, squatting next to her and placing one finger to his lips.

Even though she can't make out his face, she can tell that he is smiling. Instinctively she uses her arms to pull herself away from him. She drags her heavy legs and palms the slick surface beneath her, desperately trying to place some distance between them.

"Run," he says quietly behind her.

She tries to sob, but nothing can form in her mouth, not even a breath. The room bends and bobs, and the heat begins overwhelming her.

"Run!" he says louder now, laughing as she visibly shudders.

She shakes her head, using one hand to pull herself away. Everything is hazy now, the white room turning into a heavy curtain before her eyes. As blackness begins to close around her field of vision like a camera lens, she hears one final, terrifying sound.

"Run!" he screams.

Wren sits up in bed as light pours into her room. Her breaths come out as ragged gasps, and she is covered in a layer of slick sweat. For a moment, she can't tell if she is awake and safe from the horrific nightmare. She squints her eyes as she gazes around, trying to force her mind to acclimate. She feels her heart pounding in her chest and takes a moment to catch her breath.

"My god. That was the worst dream I have ever had," she chokes the words out to the empty bedroom, swinging her legs over the side of her bed.

She has unintentionally preempted her alarm, and notices that the window on her side of the room is allowing sunlight to pour in. The shade is askew, snagged on the slightly peeling paint. Although it shouldn't ring as significantly out of the ordinary, she can't help the paranoia she feels in the back of her mind. These Jane Does follow her home, and she is always afraid their killers will too. She shakes her head, trying to fling the intrusive thoughts from her mind. It's too early. She pulls the shade to its normal position and makes her way to the shower.

She brushes her teeth as the shower heats up, her mind wandering again. As she moves through each step of her routine, she keeps thinking about her next day off. She could really use some time away from this crop of connected bodies, discovered on every corner of her city. An entire twenty-four-hour period in which she wouldn't have to peer inside a thoracic cavity is almost a fantasy at this point. She relishes the idea of just sitting somewhere with her husband and relaxing. Hell, Richard has made that "you look a lot like my wife" joke so many times this month that she has actually started finding it kind of funny again. She blinks herself back to reality and ends her shower with a squeak of the faucet. The spa treatment is over, and it's time to get dressed for reality.

Wren waves her identification card at the sensor and pushes the heavy steel door open. A wall of slightly stale air hits her almost immediately, and she makes her way to her office.

She throws her keys down on the desk and notices the fresh stack of files taking up space in her "New Cases" bin. Sighing, she shakes her head. Typically, a heavy caseload doesn't shake her. But with news of another body found in the area and the media starting to panic the community, she is already feeling the pressure. A stack of new cases was just short of worst-case scenario.

"Can you both pop in here really quick?" Wren calls out, plopping herself into her seat. Two reliable pathology assistants come jogging into the office almost immediately. One is still in the process of tying his shoes and almost trips headfirst into a bookshelf full of anatomy atlases. He catches himself at the last moment, and Wren can see the flush of crimson flash across his cheeks. He is always so nervous.

"Hey, Dr. Muller. What can we do for you?"

"Hey. I'm going to need you to fully prep a couple of cases for me this morning," she instructs, opening the first two case files in her inbox. "It looks like we have a suspected overdose—twenty-three-year-old female found behind Tap Out. Let's make sure we get as many samples as we can from her. There are some fresh tubes with anticoagulants on the left side of the hallway closet."

The young assistant takes the file and nods. "You got it. Do you want the full organ block out?" He is already walking toward the door.

"Yes, have it prepped and out, please. I didn't notice any outward signs of trauma, but if you come across any, call me in."

Wren opens a second file and turns to the remaining pathology assistant at her door.

"For you, I have a fifty-six-year-old male. Looks like a straightforward suicide. Found in his home, gunshot wound to the roof of his mouth. No note, but you get the picture. A lefty, so make sure to test for GSR on that hand."

After delegating her less-pressing cases, Wren rises from her seat and heads into the autopsy suite.

"I'm going to catch you today," she declares out loud.

The hours in the lab fly by in a blink, and Wren is called to accompany Leroux back to the crime scene. Now she's watching him walk along the curb. They have both absorbed the profoundly negative energy surrounding this place, determined to uncover some piece of revelatory evidence in the alley next to the bar. Wren's second bachelor's degree in criminology make her an asset to these kinds of cases, both inside and outside of the autopsy suite.

Wren thinks about how frequently traveled this area is. It is hard to imagine how the killer pulled it off without being seen. It's an alley used by hundreds of people a night. It is both a quick shortcut to the streets behind the bar and a place to hide drug deals away from the bustle of the main road. But then again, no stumbling barfly with half a gallon of bourbon in their belly is going to truly take notice of their surroundings, especially when fighting their way through an alley en route to a bed. Perhaps the killer saw how simple this dump could be if he played it cool, and he did just that. Wren wants to understand the mind of mayhem. But she can see that Leroux doesn't necessarily want to understand anymore. He just wants a name.

The ground where the victim had once lain is still stained like old coffee straight from the pot. It looks as if the earth below is trying to push answers to the surface. It isn't often that Wren herself feels so helpless yet so captivated by a crime scene.

"He chose such hotel-art humans," Leroux says this without looking up.

Wren raises an eyebrow, wanting to ask him what he means. Before she can, he continues.

"Forgettable, but not invisible. Fine, but not amazing or impressive," he clarifies.

He is right. These victims were not particularly notable. They weren't highly respected members of the community, but they also weren't totally relegated to the margins of society either. No, he wasn't taking the lives of drifters or sex workers, as serial murderers of the past may have. He knows that play is almost always met with a social justice response. By the same virtue, choosing high-profile humans would fix the spotlight on him from the first drip of swamp water. So, he brilliantly chooses people who are neither princes nor paupers.

Wren pulls her hair into a bun on top of her head, twisting a hair tie tightly and smoothing out the hairs that spring free.

"They are like trees falling in the forest. They fall. Some people will genuinely care, but most will just want to collect the free firewood and move on." Leroux looks up at her. He takes a moment, pacing a little bit across the curb. He crouches down, staring at the stain on the ground before standing again.

"That would make him pretty intelligent. Malice afore-thought on a whole other level," Wren responds.

Leroux nods. "Exactly. And I think it only gets worse from here."

Wren silently agrees. It's clear to them both that the killer's actions thus far are no accident. The scene in front of them is the product of careful research, planning, and complex abstract thought.

As they turn to leave, empty-handed and enveloped in the heaviness of the crime scene, something catches Leroux's eye. It's wedged between a deep crack in the curb, where the sidewalk meets the street. He crouches down and pulls a handkerchief from his back pocket. Using it as a makeshift glove, he carefully picks a bright white business card from its place in the cement. As he lifts it to look at the front, Wren notices his face go pale. The business card is from the front desk of the medical examiner's office. Under the official seal is Wren's full name and title. Her professional contact information is across the bottom.

Wren takes a step forward, reaching a gloved hand out to hold the card herself. Leroux hands it over, a look of confusion painted across his face. She smooths her fingers over the raised OFFICE OF THE MEDICAL EXAMINER seal in the right corner. This is an old card design—Wren had painstakingly redesigned them herself about six months ago—but it's definitely hers. This card is clean, so clean that it was likely placed here recently, and intentionally. Whoever left it here did so after the victim's body was removed, and the crime scene tape was hauled away. It wasn't there when they initially arrived at the scene. They'd have noticed. Someone did this to send a message.

Wren shakes her head. "I don't like this, John. I mean it. This makes me want to run for the hills."

"Trust me, Muller, you don't have to dive off the grid just yet. We will make sure you get a security detail since it's your name on here, but, honestly, it may just be that he thinks it's clever to show us he knows how our investigations work," he reassures her, taking out an evidence bag from his pocket. He removes the card from her fingers. "And it's pretty clear he likes to scare people, specifically women."

"Ugh, John. Catch this guy so I can stop feeling so paranoid, please."

Leroux smooths out his pants and grips Wren's upper arm.

"I promise I will," he says confidently.

"I think I actually believe you."

"I'm flattered." He winks and brushes past her toward the waiting car. "Let's get this back into evidence and get away from this shit."

She nods, squeezing her eyes shut and sucking in a deep breath, just to let it out slowly before turning around to face him. "Right behind you."

CHAPTER 11

Jeremy sits in the crowded auditorium and watches her. Emily is paying close attention to the Biology lecture, taking impeccably detailed notes. Her hand never once stops moving over her notebook, and the bracelet that is almost always around her wrist jingles just slightly. The tiny, silver anatomical heart charm bounces with each pencil stroke. He imagines he is the only one who hears it. Every now and then, she nods and tips her pencil slightly forward in agreement with a particular theory. As he observes her, he feels the bubbling of anticipation again. Seeing Emily utterly oblivious to what will soon happen to her is completely tantalizing.

After three hours of lecture, it is 7:30 p.m., and he realizes that his own pen has never once touched the page. He had retreated so far into his own mind that the three hours passed like minutes. He stands up slowly, never taking his eyes off her as she gathers her things and makes her way down the row of seats to the aisle. Cracking each knuckle by his side, he steps out in front of her, plastering a friendly smile across his face. She doesn't immediately notice him in her path until he softly says her name.

"Miss Emily Maloney," he whispers, leaning close to her ear before she passes him.

Startled, she nervously chuckles, placing a hand to her chest and smiling.

"Cal!" she exclaims. "You scared the shit out of me. I swear, after three hours of this crap, I am in a complete daze."

Even after an entire semester, it still takes a moment for Jeremy to react to his alias at school. He had registered as "Cal" using fake documents. It's amazing what administrative burnout can allow to fall through the cracks. Even though he inhabited the role during school hours, he still couldn't quite get used to the name. They begin walking side by side toward the auditorium's exit as she chatters about the effects of lengthy lectures on students' cognition post-lecture. Jeremy barely hears a word. His mind is racing as he goes over the next few minutes again in his head. There is no room for error. Even the slightest hiccup would be disastrous. They round the corner, out of sight from the Biology building. He begins to carefully manipulate the rag in his right pocket around a tiny, plastic vial of chloroform.

"Do you think we can use calculators for this exam?" she asks, mindlessly scrolling through an email on her phone.

He shrugs and discreetly pokes a small hole in the plastic vial in his pocket, using a prong that was purposefully bent outward from the ring he wears on his thumb. He feels the warm liquid soak into the cloth surrounding the vial as they enter the parking garage.

"You know they will probably just give us an abacus or something. Instead of preparing us, they simply ignore the fact that modern technology is used in the real world," she continues as he clears his throat. She laughs as she takes her keys out and approaches her car door. "Well, if you want to go over the practical sheet this weekend, let me know."

He smiles and nods. "Yeah, absolutely."

A book slips from his messenger bag and hits the cement with a slap. Emily's eyes lock on it briefly as he retrieves it and shoves it back into the open bag pocket.

"What book was that? I'm looking for some good mindless reading. You know, for ten years from now when I am finally a doctor and still have no time for it." She grins widely, and he lets out an uncomfortable chuckle. He feels a little thrown and has to recalibrate.

"Oh, some horror anthology. Not exactly calming escapism." He recovers and instinctively starts to run a hand through his hair before stopping himself. "But we'll plan a study date for sure. I'll text you. Drive safe now."

"Of course. See ya, Cal."

She turns her back to open the car door, and just as quickly he takes hold of her auburn ponytail with his left hand and jams a bent knee into her upper thigh, causing her to lose her balance. He arches her head backward and covers her mouth and nose with the poison-soaked rag before she can comprehend what is happening to her. Dropping her keys, she fruitlessly claws at his hands and attempts to regain control. That's when the panic sets in.

He stares down into her wide eyes and patiently waits for complete incapacitation. When it finally comes, and her body falls limp, he throws her into the trunk of her own car and takes a quick moment to breathe and to collect his thoughts before proceeding. When his adrenaline has subsided, he snaps a glove onto his right hand, takes the vial of ketamine from his other pocket, and pulls some of it into a small syringe. Feeling around on Emily's arm for a suitable vein, he locates one and injects the dose to ensure her continued confusion when the chloroform wears off. His eyes flicker to the ground, catching a glimpse of something shiny under the bumper. Her bracelet has fallen to the concrete amid the struggle. He bends down to pick it up, examining it up close for the first time. Only now does he see the delicate letter E engraved on one side of the heart. He places the bracelet into his pocket.

As an extra precaution, he wraps a zip tie around her wrists and pulls them behind her back before he picks up her keys and sits in the driver's seat for the ride home. He lets out a long sigh and wipes his hands with a wet nap before moving a strand of box-dyed brown hair back into place in the rearview mirror. The temporary color has begun to mix with the beads of sweat on his forehead. He quickly peels off Cal's sparse beard and massages his jaw with a satisfied grin.

"Well done, Cal," he says to himself.

CHAPTER 12

"Maybe I should just stay in tonight," Wren admits as she curls the longer strands of her hair.

One piece refuses to comply, falling limply among the others like a deflated balloon. She stands in the bathroom, staring into the medicine cabinet's mirror. She's freshly showered and wearing the black, lacy "going out" shirt she bought almost a year earlier. She doesn't get out of the house much anymore, so just the act of putting on more than ChapStick marks this occasion as notable.

Richard walks out of the bedroom to her left. He has changed from his usual dress shirt and slacks into gray sweatpants and an old T-shirt. He rubs his sandy brown hair and shakes his head.

"No way," he says. "Wren, you need to go out and think about something other than work for a night. You have earned the right to relax, ya know."

"I know, but they will just ask me about work anyways. Everyone wants to hear the nasty details of the job, especially when they get a few martinis into them," she replies, curling another section of hair and fluffing the sections she has already done. "Especially my friends."

"Well, you've already gotten all dressed and dolled. You can't let it go to waste."

"I could just look nice hanging around the house tonight. Who said romance is dead? Maybe this is just how I plan to look in my downtime now." She grins, shrugging her shoulders.

"Yeah, I have always said my wife should shellac a full evening look onto her face each night to keep me happy."

"I knew it."

He leans forward, putting his face into the mirror next to hers.

"You can't bail on Lindsey's birthday."

Wren rolls her eyes in response, "All right, all right, you made your point." She finishes the last bit of hair and gives the whole thing a good shake.

Wren walks into Brennan's in a hurry. She is already late. She scans the green dining area for her friends and finally spots them among the massive crowd of people laughing and enjoying their artful plates of Louisiana seafood. Lindsey, Debbie, and Jenna sit in the rounded half booth, with Marissa sitting in a coral-pink upholstered chair opposite them. When they spot her, they wave frantically. Lindsey spills part of her drink onto Debbie with the motion, and, already, Wren feels at ease in the chaos.

"I'm so sorry I'm late, guys! I would make up an excuse, but I think you know me well enough by now."

Wren slides into the seat next to Marissa, and a collective laugh breaks out. Lindsey pushes a Bacardi and Coke garnished with a lime wedge toward Wren with a grin, motioning for her to hold it up. Her drink of choice and the only one she will enjoy tonight, since the medical examiner is always on call.

"Of course we do, and we wouldn't have it any other way. I am just so glad you came out!"

Wren clinks her glass against Lindsey's and smiles, now noticing the array of appetizers before her.

Debbie points to the oysters, beautifully spread on a plate directly in front of Wren, "Immediately try these. They will literally kill you; they are so good."

"Then you can determine your own cause of death and really launch your career to the next level."

The table erupts into tipsy laughter, and Wren can't help but smile.

"I'm always looking to better myself. So, what makes these oysters so lethal?"

"They are Oyster J'aime," Debbie says in an exaggerated French accent.

"Cornbread crumble," Jenna adds, devouring one herself.

"Say no more."

Wren eats hers without another thought and realizes her friends weren't exaggerating. Smothered in creole tomato gravy and cornbread crumble, this is an oyster she would leave Richard for on the spot.

"Oh my gosh. You somehow undersold these," she gushes, taking a sip of her drink.

The women catch up on jobs, kids, significant others, and gossip. It's comfortable. As their plates and glasses empty, Lindsey puts her hand up as if she is in class. Marissa playfully points to her as another round of laughter rolls over the table.

"Yes, Lindsey?" she calls through a chuckle.

"I want to go to a fortune-teller, guys! Can we please?" She puts her hands into a pleading position.

"Oh, absolutely." Debbie nods, grabbing her card from the bill in the center of the table.

Jenna does the same, taking a moment to quickly throw back the remains of the white wine in her glass. "Let's do it. I want to ask them about my mother-in-law's life span."

"Jenna! That's awful!" Lindsey yells a little too loudly.

Jenna shrugs with a grin. "I'm only half kidding."

Wren laughs as she stands up and grabs her clutch. "I am so in."

"Dr. Muller, did I just hear you say that you are willing, and dare I say excited, to engage in some nonsense?" Marissa teases and grabs Wren's shoulder, placing a hand over her own heart.

"Let's go to Bottom of the Cup! It's only a few minutes from here!" Debbie decides and drags her finger across her phone. She turns it for everyone to see the glowing reviews for one of the oldest and most respected tea and psychic shops in New Orleans.

"To Bottom of the Cup!" they trill in unison.

The walk is short, and the air is breezy down Conti Street and Chartres Avenue toward Bottom of the Cup. She's walked this same route hundreds of times, but always finds herself taken with the city, especially at night. The lights throw shadows on the streets. They become part of your path, like loa being called upon by a voodoo priestess. There's a cozy spookiness that covers New Orleans at night. Lush ferns and hanging plants spill from the balconies like ribbons, perfectly complimenting the intricate ironwork that the French Quarter is known for. It's only when they reach the front door of Bottom of the Cup that her friends' excited squeals break Wren from her spell.

"Hello there. I think we are all looking to get ten-minute readings, please." Lindsey gestures to the group, who nod in agreement.

The man at the counter smiles and straightens up. "Wonderful, would you like tea leaf, tarot, or palm readings tonight?"

Lindsey spins around, and polls. "What do you think, ladies?"

Wren speaks first. "I think I want tarot."

She is most familiar with a tarot reading. Even as a self-proclaimed skeptic, something about tarot cards rings more magical to her. Even if it is a load of bull, she enjoys the process, if only for the artistry and theater.

"Tarot readings for everyone, please!" Lindsey announces.

Wren slips into the black chair in the waiting area and puts her clutch on top of the table before her. These tables are famous for their impressive zodiac wheel designs.

"Anyone getting some tea while we wait?" Debbie looks up at the flavors, and Wren follows her gaze. The walls showcase dozens of tea flavors along with various metaphysical goodies that promise to set the mood just right for anyone who wishes to step into a more whimsical realm.

"Yeah, actually, tea sounds great. What are you thinking of getting?" Wren scans the names and ingredients, feeling a bit overwhelmed by the choices and flavor combinations.

"I am stuck between the Monk's Blend and Buckingham Palace Garden Party," Debbie answers, giggling a little.

"Oh, definitely Buckingham Palace Garden Party, if only for the name," she decides, finding it on the list. "Also, jasmine and cornflower petals sound too pretty to pass up."

Debbie nods, walking toward the counter again. Before she returns, a beautiful older woman strolls out from the back of the shop. Her hair is tightly tied up on her head, and her cheekbones rival Bowie's. Beside her, a middle-aged man emerges. He has kind eyes and a clean-shaven face, with wild blond curls spilling out from the top of his head.

"Evening. I am Martine. We can do two at a time," the statuesque woman explains. "One of you can come with me, and the other one can go with Leo here." She gestures to the man next to her and then holds her hand out to usher someone forward.

Lindsey jumps to her feet, grabbing Wren's hand as she does.

"Let's go before this one falls asleep. This is the latest she has been out without a homicide involved in months."

"My tea!" Wren protests.

Debbie rushes over, thrusting a to-go cup in Wren's hand. "I got you covered." She winks, and Wren purses her lips.

"Thanks, friend," she mocks before standing up to surrender.

Martine lightly touches Wren's arm, showing her where to go. She leads her down a small hallway and into a door on the right. Inside, there is a black table with a small green lamp resembling an antique candelabra. A large gold-framed mirror is over the table on the wall, and a stack of tarot cards sits in the center.

"Please, make yourself comfortable." Martine smiles, pulling Wren's chair out for her as she settles in across the table. "Shall I record the audio of this reading for you to take with you when we are done?"

"Thank you, that would be great."

Wren sits, pulling her chair into the table and taking in the light spa-like music playing softly in the background. She leans forward to admire the intricate designs on the back of the top card in the stack. Martine smiles softly to herself, reaching for them gently.

"Beautiful, aren't they? They are very old. Passed down to me by my grandmother. These cards hold a lot of history."

Martine pauses a moment before looking back up into Wren's eyes. They lock together before she pushes the cards to the side. "Would you be open to a brief palm reading before we look at the cards?"

She seems compelled into the suggestion, and Wren nods wordlessly. As skeptical as she is about the lines of her hand telling a story, she is too curious to refuse.

Martine takes her hand in her own and turns it over, studying her palm and using her fingers to stretch the lines out for better viewing.

"You see this? Like a natural ring?" she asks, tracing her own finger over the small, arched line under Wren's index finger. She strains her eyes to see it, but it's there.

"Yes. It does look a little bit like a ring."

"It's called the Ring of Solomon. It tells me that you are a leader. You are strong, independent, and highly intelligent. It also tells me that sometimes these traits can run your life. Your work and success stifle your more creative impulses," Martine offers. Wren can't help but feel exposed.

How can a line under her finger tell this woman all of that?

Martine grins, twisting Wren's hand another way.

"This line," she continues, pointing to a very faint line extending across the middle of her palm from the bottom of her pinky to the space between her index finger and thumb. "This line is unique. It's the Simian Line."

Wren sees it faintly but makes sure she looks at Martine's face to study her expression. Martine furrows her brows together before clasping her other hand on top of Wren's, almost in a show of comfort.

"This line tells me that you have a hard time viewing life in abstract ways. You see black and white. But not gray. Your analytical nature is your greatest asset, but also I have a strong feeling that this is something detrimental to your current situation."

Wren can feel her mouth open of its own accord.

"And what situation is that?" She can't believe she is indulging Martine.

"Let's see if the cards will tell me," Martine responds calmly, handing the stack to Wren. "Use your left hand and cut this stack into two piles. Cut the stack where you feel the strongest urge to do so."

Wren does as she is told but doesn't feel anything, so she cuts it at random, placing the cards facedown on the table. Martine pulls a card from the top of each stack, turning them over and placing them on the table in front of them.

Both cards face Martine. The Moon and the High Priestess. She lightly places her hands over both the cards, looking into Wren's face.

"These cards face me, or, more importantly, they face away from you, which changes their meaning," Martine begins and breaks her gaze, bringing her eyes to the cards. "The Moon is telling you to listen to your inner voice. You are receiving messages, but you are blocking them. I would imagine, from what your hands told me, that it is your analytical nature that makes you less open to these answers."

Wren isn't sure what to think about this reading so far.

"The High Priestess card," Martine continues. "This is interesting. It's another about trusting one's intuition, but for you this card also is telling me that secrets surround you. Someone in your life now or in the past embroiled you in a secret that you may not fully understand."

Wren racks her brain trying to connect these ideas of messages and secrets, but she feels nothing but confusion. Martine pushes the two cut stacks together and shuffles them once more. She holds the stack out to Wren and finally meets her eyes.

"Please take a card from this deck."

Her voice is soft, but there is a force behind her instruction. Wren wordlessly pulls a card from the middle of the deck, handing it back to Martine, who flips it over onto the table. As the card hits the surface, Martine brings her hand up to her mouth, resting her index finger onto her bottom lip.

"The Ten of Swords," she announces and places her finger onto the card, showing Wren the illustrated man lying on his stomach with ten long swords protruding from his back. The card is haunting and ominous, even without an explanation.

"Betrayal," Martine whispers before looking back up. "He's done something horrible."

The words hit Wren hard. "Who? Who has done something horrible?"

Martine shakes her head. "You know who. Follow your intuition," she advises, touching the Moon and High Priestess cards again.

Wren's breath hitches in her throat.

"How?" she asks quietly, leaning forward slightly.

Martine swallows, shaking her head again. "You know how. It's all there for you. Stop him."

They hold each other's gaze. Wren's head swims with questions, and her heart feels like it may never slow to its resting rhythm. Then, as if on cue, the sharp sound of porcelain shattering from the front of the shop breaks the silence. Wren stands quickly, almost knocking her chair over in the process.

"Thank you, Martine," she blurts out.

She spins around and quickly walks out the door and into the hallway. When she turns to glance back, Martine is still sitting at the table, her hands on the cards.

"How was it? You look like you saw a ghost. So, I'm guessing, amazing?" Jenna asks, bent over to pick up pieces of a shattered teacup. "We had a party foul out here."

Wren feels like she is in a fog. She grabs her clutch from the zodiac wheel table.

"It was really great. I just have to get going," she says hurriedly.

"Oh no, called into work?" Marissa stands as Leo brings Lindsey out from the back.

"Noooo! Someone died on my birthday?" she complains. Wren gives her a quick hug.

"Unfortunately, yes," she lies. "Happy birthday, hun. This was so fun. I am so glad I came out to celebrate with you."

She pulls a forced smile onto her face and turns to leave.

"Wren!" Martine's voice calls. She's holding a small square envelope in her hand. "Your recording."

Wren takes in another sharp breath, meeting her halfway to take it.

"Thank you, Martine."

As she leaves, she looks back briefly to see Martine nod. She grips her clutch and makes her way to her car, trying desperately to shake this feeling from her head.

It's fake. A lucky guess. She probably has seen me in the press or something.

She shoves the CD into her clutch and slides into the driver's seat.

I should have just stayed home.

Wren finds herself idling outside a bar not too far down the road and by chance spots Leroux standing outside. She watches him make his way toward the bar's front door, only stopping briefly to take a drag from his cigarette. He exhales smoke into the cool night air, and Wren watches as the cloud of poison spirals with the light breeze. The smoke dances a bit before it dissipates into the atmosphere, and she feels calm for a moment as she watches it disappear. When she looks back at Leroux, it's clear that he too needed an escape, if only for a second.

"So sorry, sweetie!" A young woman slams into Leroux's arm, making him stumble. She's apologizing through giggles and fighting to stay upright in sky-high heels.

Wren can't help but laugh at the scene. She throws her car into park and follows Leroux inside. His partner on the force of two years, Detective William Broussard, is already stationed on a bar stool, apparently having put down roots at the bar counter hours before, judging by the tumbler of amber-colored alcohol half gone in front of him.

"Hello, boys," she announces, scooting over a stool to sit beside them.

"Muller! Surprised to see you in this neck of the woods. And at this hour. Isn't it past your bedtime?" Leroux responds, smiling cheekily.

"Ha ha. I was just driving by and saw you out front. Figured I'd not let the coincidence go to waste."

Will hasn't taken his eyes off the television that sits high above the shelves of alcohol.

"Can you believe this shit still gets steam?" he asks, gesturing with a nod to the news story playing out on the screen.

Leroux and Wren raise their eyes to the screen and follow his gaze. The local news is highlighting a middle-aged man interviewed by a young, eager reporter. The man looks frazzled and wrings his hands anxiously while he talks.

"It is the occult. Devil worshippers are infiltrating this community, and until we get back to respecting the teachings of Jesus Christ, more innocent people will be sacrificed to the darkness," the man on the screen proselytizes.

He raises his hand during the last few words, and the reporter nods enthusiastically along with his sermon. The camera then switches to another interview with a larger group of concerned citizens, wearing an astonishing array of novelty T-shirts, baseball hats, and jean shorts. The group is frenzied, hyping one another up behind a man with a microphone.

"This community is in danger of falling prey to the ways of the devil!" he yells. "Our children are next! Don't you get it? These disciples of Satan will tear them from their beds and sacrifice them to their master! The cops need to round these freaks up and toss them into the swamp. Why are the good people of Orleans Parish the only ones who see that this is the work of a group of devil worshippers?"

The reporter, who has tried to interject a couple of times, finally asks, "So, you think the recent murders are not isolated incidents, as has been stated by law enforcement?"

The crowd incoherently yells their answers, and their unofficial spokesman nods aggressively.

"The police are lying to us! They don't want us to know how deep the occult has embedded itself in this community. This is the work of the devil and his followers. Mark my words!"

Leroux chuckles and turns away from the screen, pointing to Will's drink as the bartender approaches. "Whatever this is, please."

She smiles and nods, taking a glass tumbler out from below the bar and filling it with Macallan twelve single malt scotch.

"Cheers." He salutes and holds his glass up, and Wren mimes clinking an invisible glass with his.

Will shakes his head and takes a sip from his own glass. "This satanic panic stuff was supposed to die out at some point, right? It's the eighties all over again and completely acceptable to assume angry goths are committing sophisticated murders."

"Bound to happen." Leroux sighs.

Will raises one eyebrow and turns to look at him. "Are we really at the point where we are just accepting a complete breakdown of rational thought?"

Leroux shrugs slightly as he takes a sip of drink.

"Well, kind of." He gestures at the screen up above them. "People look for patterns that aren't there because they are scared shitless. They can't handle that they are just as likely to be scooped up by a totally normal-looking psychopath as the victims were, so they make up this crap instead."

"I hate when you make sense." Will shakes his head and leans back in his seat. "The problem is these people are redirecting the focus now. Instead of looking for the single, basement-dwelling asshole responsible for these weird crime scenes, they are encouraging people to start tackling anyone in a Metallica T-shirt."

"Yeah, and these news stations are giving them a shiny new platform for their bullshit."

"Ugh, I can't talk about this anymore." Will pivots, "Still nothing on that paper he left with the book?"

Leroux shakes his head. "Nada. Ben is hitting walls left and right over there."

"This guy definitely thinks he is smarter than everyone around him. And no doubt, he is loving all of this." Will sneers, gesturing again at the screen.

Leroux nods, puckering his lips a bit. "I agree that he thinks he's smarter than everyone, but I actually would put money on the idea that he's pissed about this Satan stuff."

"Yeah? I'd think he'd be psyched to have the heat off him. People aren't going to be looking for a Ted Bundy–type anymore. These fools have them worrying about Charles Manson and the family."

"I just don't think he is that simpleminded. At least, based on his profile."

"You think?" Will asks incredulously. "I guess I have to believe your weird ass on this one."

Leroux laughs and leans forward, planting his elbows on the bar. "Yeah, well, let's hope I'm not way off base here. To me, he just seems like a classically organized killer. Wren, want to tell Will the latest chapter in this guy's rise up the ranks of enormity?"

Will sighs and drops his head dramatically. "I have a feeling I don't want to know."

"That last body? He refrigerated it," Wren interjects finally.

"Wait, what? Refrigerated? Why?"

"It really messes with getting an accurate time of death. Throws off the progression of livor mortis or something," Leroux cuts in.

"Wow, well done. You angling for my job or something?" Wren teases.

Will just shakes his head as he asks, "He didn't do this with the other one, right?"

"Nope. Just this latest," Wren confirms.

Leroux glances up at the mirror, blinks, and narrows his gaze determinedly. He stands and turns to face the bustling bar, his eyes wild but focused.

"What are you looking at?" Will swivels himself around and cranes his neck.

Leroux walks straight through groups of people, slamming into someone's drink as he passes.

"Hey, asshole!" the stranger calls after him, raising his hands in frustration and wiping his button-down shirt.

Leroux ignores him and doesn't stop until he stands in front of the wall just to the right of the entrance. Wren squints, watching both ends of the bar. She can make out the stark white flyer thumbtacked on the dark brown wood paneling that has caught Leroux's attention. It's an advertisement for an upcoming jazz festival on Bourbon Street—a prelude to Mardi Gras season and a considerable crowd draw. She watches as Leroux reaches out and touches it, feeling the embossed fleur-de-lis border. It has a sheen to it, iridescent.

Exactly like the scrap paper left with the last body.

CHAPTER 13

J EREMY WATCHES EMILY WAKE THROUGH the monitor screen, her head no doubt pounding as she flutters her eyes open. She tries desperately to blink out the haze that comes from the chloroform-and-ketamine cocktail, quickly realizing that she is surrounded by pitch blackness and sitting in something moist and spongy.

She's probably wondering why she is outside. But before she can contemplate her situation too deeply, the sharp sound of audio feedback echoes high in the darkness, jolting her to her feet. She scrambles to gain her balance and blinks to find the source but is startled again when Jeremy's voice begins to speak.

"Good evening, guests. I would love it if you all could give me your attention for a moment."

Does she recognize my voice yet?

"Somewhere near each of you, there should be a flashlight. Use it. I don't need anyone accidentally drowning in a swamp out here."

Emily scans the ground around her, moving her face close to the moss and roots that creep under her feet. It's almost funny to watch from Jeremy's vantage point. His night-vision camera bathes everything in a green light, making Emily look like an alien creature shoving her face into the ground. In reality, she can't even see her own nose in front of her. She blindly feels the surface beneath her, finding only swampy earth before her foot hits something foreign and solid. It's the flashlight.

"You have been dropped in random locations on my property. There is a fence around the perimeter, and speakers have been mounted in various places within it."

She must know by now.

Her face changes. It's complete recognition. It is the voice of her lab partner broadcasting through the speakers. It is the voice of the last person she remembers seeing before she opened her eyes out here.

With a satisfied smile, he continues into the speaker, "Look, this game is simple. Your only job is to do your best to evade me as I make my way through the course. It's that easy. The name of the game is to survive, my friends. Try to escape, if you can. The only thing between you and your freedom is a few acres of bayou . . . and me."

She clicks on her flashlight. The beam of light casts forward to reveal that a blanket of moss surrounds her. The low-hanging branches of what looks like a thousand bald cypress trees reach around her like hungry predators. She is so alone, but he has made sure she feels suffocated. Her chest heaves, and she lets out a childlike sob.

"Don't worry, I'm a fair guy. I gave you a generous head start. And don't forget to take it all in. This may well be your last few hours as a sentient bag of flesh."

Emily lurches forward as a paralyzing fear visibly ignites her nervous system. For a second, Jeremy thinks she may just break. Instead, she takes a deep breath in and closes her eyes. Her face turns almost calm. Using her newfound flashlight, she starts taking inventory of her own skin.

She's looking for marks. Smart girl.

She spots something—the small bruise that is almost certainly tender on her arm. He can tell she knows she has been drugged. When she looks down at her feet, at her beat-up moccasins, a snake large enough for Jeremy to see on camera slithers past her foot, and she cries out in frustration. The canopy of trees blocks out any light from the moon, and the interminable sound of cicadas keep her senses on edge. Sound can manipulate emotions better than almost anything else. Somewhere an owl calls out, and she jumps slightly. He brings the microphone back to his lips.

"Let's get started. My advice? Run."

He hesitates for a second, but she doesn't. She runs. Tripping over uneven terrain and twisted cypress roots, she frantically searches for safety. And suddenly another sound cuts through the darkness, making her cover her ears.

Music. He starts to play music.

CHAPTER 14

WREN ENTERS THE CRIME LABORATORY through the staff entrance. She walks down the hallway quickly, her heels clicking on the newly renovated floor, and makes her way toward the office where Leroux told her to meet him.

As she rounds the corner, she sees Leroux inside on the phone. By the smile on his face, she can tell it's a personal call with Andrew.

"I really am sorry about the cream. I know you hate it when I leave the empty container in the fridge like an asshole," Leroux sheepishly admits.

Andrew's loud voice carries through the phone enough for Wren to make out almost everything he is saying.

"John, it's fine. I know this case has you strung out lately."

He can't fully comprehend what Leroux's job requires of him, especially lately. He's an executive chef at a high-end restaurant in New Orleans, working similarly absurd hours, but the type of stress is incomparable. Picky customers and incompetent line workers can make for a tough shift and a shitty Yelp rating, but bearing witness to the horrors that human beings willingly inflict upon one another burrows far deeper. But he tries to empathize, and that's what matters.

"Yeah, it's just been kind of a weird one, and I feel like I'm letting my dad down or something."

"Don't get mopey now. You have a job to do." Andrew's words are almost like a pat on the back, and Wren watches as Leroux's face softens. "And you're on the right track after finding that flyer."

"Yeah, yeah. You're right."

"But next time there's no cream for my coffee, I won't be so understanding."

Wren can't help it, she laughs through her hand, startling Leroux. He looks up and smiles, shaking his head and throwing Andrew on speakerphone. "Andrew, say hi to Muller."

"Hi, Wren!" Andrew yells loudly over the speaker.

"Hi, Andrew! How's my favorite chef in all of Louisiana?" Wren grins, taking a seat.

"Oh, you know, taking the culinary world by storm and keeping my broody boyfriend at bay."

Wren looks over at Leroux, who is rolling his eyes. He leans over and spins the speaker back in his direction. "All right, enough chitchat for one day. See you at home, Andrew."

"Every party has a pooper; that's why we invited you," Andrew manages to say before being cut off.

Wren laughs again, spinning around in the chair to look at the office they are in. "I love Andrew."

"Yeah, he's a peach. Anyways, let's get into it. The flyer. I still can't get over it. I'm telling you, it was like fate. I saw it in a fucking mirror!" Leroux is animated, his eyes on fire with exhaustion and excitement. "It's for that jazz festival this weekend. Embellishments, color, and type match the scrap exactly."

Wren stands up. "I assume we have a meeting with Ben?"

They enter the laboratory area where Ben sits on a stool by a lab bench. He's tall and lanky, with round, wire-rimmed glasses and black hair that is shaved cleanly to his head. Next to him is Leroux's partner, Will, waiting impatiently with his hands shoved into his pockets.

"So?" Leroux asks eagerly as they approach, his arms outstretched.

"It is definitely the same paper. You can see that both are recycled with bits of salvage distributed evenly throughout the page, and it has the same sheen that the original had," Ben explains as he lines up the scrap of paper that was left near the victim's body with the flyer from the bar to punctuate his point.

Leroux and Will can't help but mirror Ben's proud grin.

Wren interrupts the celebratory spirit. "Do you think he's already killed the new victim, or is he still scouting for this drop?"

"There's no way to know for sure. I don't think we can stop something from happening here; we can only prepare for what is coming," Leroux answers, now solemn.

Wren looks off and shakes her head. "He is a real piece of work, this one."

"The Bayou Butcher returns," Ben throws out flippantly.

Wren stops abruptly, turning quickly to face the group. "The Bayou Butcher?"

Ben looks from Wren to Leroux, sensing he has said too much. "You know, the brutally violent methods, the swamp water . . ."

Wren quickly walks into the hallway, spotting a water-cooler and making a beeline for it. As she sips it from the tiny paper cup, her thoughts jumble like weeds. Composing herself quickly, she rejoins the group. "Sorry, dehydration emergency."

Leroux quirks an eyebrow in her direction as if making a mental note to check up on her later.

He continues, "Well, now we have a time and place, let's get a plan rolling here. The festival is only hours away. I'll bring this to the station and see what higher-ups want to do. Muller, you coming?"

"You had me at Butcher," she says as she walks through the open door in front of them.

Wren is suddenly even more thankful to be the boss at the ME's office. As they enter the police station together, she feels the atmosphere become heavier somehow. The smell of stale coffee and frustration wafts through the air like a humid breeze.

The lieutenant is intimidating at first glance. He is physically looming, with thick arms, a bald head, and gray eyes that can bring anyone to their knees. Standing somewhere around six foot three, he was made for a position of power.

And at this particular moment, he is looking over the papers and reports that were thrust into his face first thing this morning. Leroux and Will didn't waste a second sharing the news of their newly discovered evidentiary connection. They had burst into his office, both speaking over each other in a haze of exhaustion and adrenaline until he held up one of his massive hands and demanded silence, and the space to read over what they just threw on his desk. Now, Leroux can see the wheels turning in the lieutenant's head as he pieces together exactly what needs to be done next.

"So, you think it's a body drop?" he asks, flicking his eyes up to meet Leroux's and Will's. He briefly eyes Wren but gives her a nod of approval quickly.

Leroux nods and leans forward with his elbows on his knees. He answers, "That is exactly what I think."

"Should we try to have the festival canceled? Is that even possible this late in the game?" Will questions.

The lieutenant shakes his head and leans back in his chair, responding, "No way. Technically, it has already begun. There are hundreds of people converging on New Orleans as we speak. It's an all-day event."

Leroux points to the flyer and clarifies, "This advertisement is specifically referring to the events beginning at four p.m."

"So, there is time to get people out of there. We really don't know the extent of what he has planned. The best-case scenario is a body drop, but we could be looking at something much worse," Will adds, concerned.

"An evacuation might cause mass chaos," Wren interjects, holding up a finger for emphasis.

"Dr. Muller is right. Any move like that is going to spook him. If this asshole has something planned tonight, he will notice if the place starts emptying out prematurely. Besides, a mass exodus would cause chaos and panic. This community is already on edge. They don't need to be chased away by a ghost," the lieutenant decides, stroking his chin and feeling the flyer between his fingers. He stands and walks around the other side of his desk. "Let's get a team together. I want every officer we can get on this. Hell, let's get the administrative team suited up. I want that festival surrounded in rows, like shark's teeth. No one moves without eyes on them. If people have an issue with it, remind them that there is a possible serial killer turning people into pulled pork."

Leroux turns to Wren and instructs, "Muller, grab your team to come with us for this."

The lieutenant nods and passes through the door of his office, agreeing, "Absolutely. Get them on the phone. We need you on the scene right from the jump."

"Of course. I'll get them rolling now." Wren pulls out her phone and sends texts to the members of her team she wants to summon.

She follows Leroux and Will into the hallway, listening to them fill in a few officers nearby. In what seems like an instant, the scene inside the station has changed from business as usual to a state of heightened urgency.

"Get in here, Leroux. We don't have time to waste staring into the abyss." The lieutenant waves a giant hand and disappears into the conference room.

Leroux walks into the conference room with Wren follow-ing close behind. Everyone is buzzing. The air feels thick with equal parts adrenaline and nervous energy. The lieutenant's booming voice cuts through it like a machete.

"Here it is," the lieutenant declares, slapping the jazz festival flyer onto the bulletin board that has been wheeled in front of the room. He stabs a tack into it and turns to face the group. "This is where the killer responsible for the Seven Sisters Swamp and Twelve Mile Limit murder scenes will likely be tonight. If his own breadcrumbs are to be believed, he plans to ruin more innocent people's lives. Leroux and Broussard, get up here."

Leroux and Will exchange an anxious look but follow the orders of their superior. The room has started to dissolve into chaos as the news washes over everyone at once. Leroux hates standing in front of a room. Wren can already see the red splotches appear on his collarbone. He, like she, prefers the solitude of research and individual legwork to the immense pressure of sharing vital information with a large group. Leroux clears his throat and gestures somewhat broadly to the flyer stuck to the bulletin board.

"So, we have found a pretty definitive match for the piece of paper found on the last victim's body. It is from this flyer for the jazz festival downtown today. Based on what we have dis-covered to be an emerging pattern across these crime scenes, it is extremely likely that there will be a body drop at the festival or somewhere around it."

A young patrolman raises a finger in the air and lets his elbow drop on the arm of his chair with a clear sense of skepticism. "How the hell is this guy going to even consider dropping a dead body at a huge festival? So far, he has been doing his drops at night. Are we supposed to believe he has suddenly escalated to this level of confidence?" he asks as his face twists into a look of exasperation.

Will pipes right up before Leroux can.

"Listen, no one is saying that we know exactly what his plan will be. If we knew that, we would already have our own television show, and no one else would die," he jokes.

The room snickers and the heckler turns his head to the side in a snarl. Leroux grins, too, but quickly returns his focus to the situation in front of him. Wren can see that he wants to say more. She wishes he would.

"All we know is that all signs point to something big happening at the festival. Now, whether it is a false alarm or a prank is not really pertinent here. We can't take the risk, and I don't think anyone will fault us for acting in a massive way here," Leroux confirms.

The room seems to agree that overreacting is highly preferable to possibly risking more lives. The lieutenant uses a deep, stern voice to silence the mumbling. "This is priority number one now. Everyone is to have their eyes open and their radar up at this event. If I see a phone in one of your hands tonight, I'll make you eat it," he warns.

Snickers fill the room again, followed by anxious chatter as Leroux and Will begin to explain the plan of attack. Will smooths out a map of the festival site and tacks it up on the board.

"There are three stages set up out there now. One main guy and two smaller ones," Will explains, pointing to the three sections on the map. "Obviously, most of the crowd will gather around these areas, as well as the spots where food is sold. People love to eat, and they love to listen to loud local music up close. We will station most of you around these high-traffic zones and then stagger the coverage throughout the rest of the festival grounds."

Leroux nods along in approval, clasping his hands together and bringing them to his chin. "Every single entrance and exit has to be covered and then covered some more. No one gets in and no one gets out without us knowing about it," he adds.

Wren can see the skepticism on some of the faces in the room and knows Leroux sees it too. Even she can't help the questions forming in her own mind. Is the killer really this brazen? Is he really this stupid? His confidence level has always seemed higher than most, even from his first body dump. It isn't entirely out of the realm of possibility that he is capable of escalating to this grand show of power. But she also wonders if Leroux's plan and legions of officers will actually help today. This killer is the type of guy who blends in. He doesn't make civilians cross the street to avoid him or clasp their purses tighter as they pass by. He doesn't wear his evil on his sleeve or even his face. Based on his profile, she believes he was able to convince most of his victims to leave with him willingly. He didn't forcibly abduct them. He is interested in causing chaos from afar, not becoming entrenched in it himself.

Wren scans the room with more unease than she had when she walked in.

CHAPTER 15

JEREMY HITS A BUTTON ON his phone and props the speaker by the microphone. The playlist that he meticulously put together for this night begins to sound through the darkness, and he smiles with anticipation. He steps out from the shed that houses his audio equipment and takes a second to pour some water on one of his thirsty magnolia bushes, gently passing the delicate white petals between his fingers. He breathes in the crisp night air and moves his shoulders with the music. David Bowie's "Suffragette City" echoes across the acres of isolated swampland, and he checks his tools one last time. He lightly touches the Glock 22 tucked into the holster around his midsection and pats the cargo pocket on his right pant leg to confirm that it still holds the seventeen-inch serrated hunting knife. Tugging on the shotgun slung across his back, he takes his time walking into the abyss of trees that stretches out before him.

Growing up, his family stifled his curiosity. He wasn't encouraged to pursue the things that interested him most. His penchant for exploring the inner workings of small animals through dissection made people uncomfortable. And after his father died, he grew even more resentful of his mother and the ways in which she held him back from reaching his true potential. That is why he felt such a long-awaited sense of relief years ago when he freed himself from her. Now his curiosities are unfettered, and he is free to play for as long as he wishes.

He wonders whether his other guests listened when he instructed them to run. Assuming they are moving and not stuck to the ground in fear, they'll probably find one another at some point tonight. That might make things a little messy. He doesn't love mess, but sometimes he accepts it as inevitable. Ducking under Spanish moss and slipping the night-vision goggles onto his face, he steps over twisted roots and scans the woods in front of him. When nothing appears, he unlocks his phone. The app connects to the various security cameras nestled around the property and flicks to life at his command. He taps through the various angles until he lands on one that shows Emily in the darkness.

The dizzying sounds of the night mix with the upbeat music. He can see Emily pressing her back against a cypress tree and sticking her fingers in her ears. As he watches her struggle to catch her breath and adjust her eyes to the darkness, he wonders what thoughts are running through her head. She scans the area around her, probably wondering whether he is close. Just as he begins to tire of her, she moves forward. She's going to make him work for it. Now she is moving across the swampy ground, keeping her pace brisk and her flashlight use minimal. He has to tap through more angles just to keep up with her. His own pulse quickens at the challenge.

Suddenly, she stops. He sees her turn her attention to her left side and stop dead in her tracks. Clicking off her light, she waits and tries to hear through the cacophony of sounds. Jeremy hears what put her on edge. The snap of a branch must feel a million miles away and right on top of her at the same time. Suddenly, a stream of light encases her.

"Who are you?" a panicked, decidedly female voice squeaks out from behind the flashlight.

Emily lets out the breath, and Jeremy can see her whole body shudder.

"Emily. I'm Emily," she stammers, placing a hand on her chest and closing her eyes to block out the harsh light.

The light lowers, and there is an audible sigh of relief from its owner.

"Oh, thank god." Katie closes her tired eyes and squats down, steadying herself on a tree with a hand that is caked in old blood. Emily's eyes draw to the sight like a moth to a flame.

"Who are you?" Emily clicks on her own flashlight, casting a spotlight on Jeremy's irritating guest.

"Katie. But introductions hardly even matter right now," she snaps. "He's just going to kill us anyway. Super psyched to meet you though!" She rubs her forehead and starts to cry softly.

Pathetic.

Emily shakes her head. "He isn't going to kill me."

Katie chuckles slightly and brings herself to her feet. "Sure. Listen, you just got here. We have been with him for days. Where did he get you?"

Jeremy can't help but smile.

"Cal is my lab partner. We're in the same grad program." She twitches her head from side to side, ever vigilant.

"Who is Cal? Is he out here too?" Katie looks confused and frustrated.

Jeremy laughs out loud.

Emily quirks a brow, flicking her eyes to the side. "He's the one who's doing all this. I thought you said you had spent days with him."

She looks confused too. Jeremy is delighted.

Katie is visibly annoyed. "I don't know who the hell Cal is, but this guy's name is Jeremy."

"Whatever you say. Listen, who else is out here? Is there anyone else?" Emily asks.

He can see the panic return to Emily's face as she considers the possibility that there are more of him around her.

Katie softly whimpers, utterly exhausted. "My friend Matt. He should be around here somewhere. Unless Jeremy already found him."

Emily takes an audible sharp breath in and looks around.

"All right, Katie. We have to move. Let's try to find Matt," she declares.

He sees the light of Katie's flashlight dim slightly. Emily can see it too.

"You should probably turn off your flashlight." She gestures toward the dimming beam of Katie's light.

Katie chuckles mockingly and shakes her head.

"No way. I have been in a pitch-black basement for days. Why the hell would I want to stumble around in the dark out here too?"

Emily bites at her lip and tries to maintain her composure as she explains, "Well, the way it's dimming, you won't have a choice pretty soon."

Her voice is sharp and aggravated.

Katie flips the light to shine into her own face and shrugs. "Like I said, he's not going to let us go, and I'm not dying in the dark."

Emily concedes and walks after her.

The song ends. Emily and Katie both look up into the sky with relief. Then, without warning, Van Morrison's "Moondance" begins to fill the darkness, causing them both to jump a bit at the surprise. As they trudge through the thick brush, ducking under slimy Spanish moss and sinking into the ankle-deep swamp with every step, he can see Emily struggling to stay alert through the smothering sounds of the Louisiana bayou and sickeningly jovial music.

"What was that?" She stops moving and cranes her neck to sift through the chaos.

Jeremy is moving now. He slithers slowly and quietly toward them. He remains far enough away to stay out of sight, but close enough to observe the scene with his own senses. Katie freezes and spins her light in every direction, much to Emily's obvious chagrin.

"Matt?" she calls out too loudly.

Emily grabs Katie and throws her hand over her mouth, hushing her aggressively.

"What if Cal hears you?!" she whispers harshly in her ear, loud enough for Jeremy to hear.

He's smiling now. It's like watching a show. He didn't anticipate it would play out so seamlessly. Katie and Emily have embodied their roles like actors on a stage.

Katie peels her hand away, shooting Emily an angry look and dropping her light to her side. "What if it's Matt?" she snarls.

Emily puts a finger up to silence her again and cranes her head to listen. The familiar click of metal on metal. Jeremy pumps his shotgun loudly, becoming a part of the performance.

"Get down!" Emily screeches, dropping to the ground while pulling Katie into a crumpled heap next to her.

Emily instinctively covers her head, and Katie squeals as she flops into the mud like a rag doll. Just as they hit the swampy land beneath them, Jeremy's shot hits the tree behind them, creating an explosion of bark and smoke.

Emily knows that blast. She once told Cal that her father taught her about weaponry of all kinds while she was growing up. While she never found herself interested in owning guns, the knowledge still remains.

"Fight or flight, girls. Fight or flight," Jeremy whispers to himself.

His eyes never leave the scene before him. He feels their fear from where he stands. It's like a tide washing in, filling the air with the scent of panic and desperation.

"Go, Katie! Go!" Emily shoves Katie forward, keeping low to the ground and choosing flight.

Katie sobs and stumbles forward, covering her own head with her hands and creating a commotion.

"Katie, you have to be quiet and fucking move!" she angrily spits out.

I knew she would hate Katie.

Jeremy paired them together for a reason, and he's pleased with the animosity blooming between them.

Katie shakes her head, sobbing and paralyzed on her hands and knees.

"I can't! I can't do it!" she wails.

Emily moves next to her in an instant, throwing her arm around her neck and cupping her own hand over Katie's mouth. Without a word, she begins dragging her along at a brisk pace. Jeremy moves swiftly alongside them, relishing the power that comes from seeing someone who can't see you. Pushing hard through the sea of trees, they finally stop to rest, Emily nearly collapsing from exhaustion.

"We can't stay here long." Emily pants, placing her hands on her hips and squinting into the darkness around them. "We are sitting ducks if we don't keep moving."

Katie shakes her head.

"Where the fuck are we going to go?" She throws her hands up before slapping them back down into the mud. "It's us against a psycho with a gun. We're going to run around like idiots until he shoots us from a fucking tree or something. We should stay here and hide until morning."

"That's your plan? You really think he will just leave when the sun comes up?" Emily squeezes her eyes shut and bends forward.

"He said we just had to evade him. That's all we have to do."

Emily isn't the type to leave someone behind, even if they irritate her to no end. She's a hero in her own mind, Jeremy knows.

"You honestly trust this guy's word? You think someone with the patience to hide you away for days and befriend me for months will just give up because we hid from him for a few hours?"

Katie shrugs, and Emily brushes a spider off her shoulder with a sigh.

"So, you don't want to find your friend out here? You want to leave Matt to die alone?"

Jeremy is fascinated. Her survival instinct is so strong, yet she's willing to ignore it to help this delusional stranger.

"He's probably already dead."

"Well, we are not going to die out—" Emily stops.

Branches snap. And they both hear a shuffle of feet. Katie looks up at Emily with wide, terrified eyes. Gripping the tree trunk behind her, Emily holds her breath, desperately trying to see her surroundings.

Not me this time, friends.

Jeremy smirks to himself, waiting for the next arrival.

"Katie!" a hushed male voice sounds out from the darkness.

Katie gets to her feet and reaches for her flashlight.

"Oh my god, Matt?!" she whispers back in what sounds like pure disbelief.

The flashlight clicks on, and a stream of light casts out across the trees. A disheveled man in dirty clothes stands twenty feet away. A smile spreads across his face, and Katie bursts into relieved laughter. Emily lets out her breath and steps out from her hiding spot. They begin walking toward one another, letting their guards down. Jeremy shakes his head at their insipidity and raises his Glock, aiming it toward their gathering spot.

"I can't believe we found you!" Katie runs forward to jump into a hug with Matt, who grimaces in pain.

"Yeah, I was sure I wouldn't be able to walk on this knee, but I guess adrenaline took over."

Emily looks down at Matt's right knee, crusted in old blood and fresh mud. Her eyes betray her terror, suddenly compounded by a loud pop that seems to come out of nowhere. A bullet from Jeremy's handgun rips into Matt's temple, spraying drops of blood onto Katie's face. He drops to the ground like a bird that's been shot mid-flight, and Katie screams. But before Katie can process the grisly scene, Emily grabs her arm and starts running.

"Best of luck, ladies and . . . well, actually, *just* ladies now." Jeremy grins, tucking the handgun back into its holster.

CHAPTER 16

ALL AT ONCE, LIKE AN unpredictable hemorrhage, Wren can smell it.

It's subtle. So subtle that she wonders if it is just an olfactory hallucination, a result of too many morgue hours. To an untrained nose, it could smell like a foul plate of festival food or a street meat experiment gone awry. But Wren knows it is the unmistakable stench of early decomposition in stiflingly hot weather.

The smell always starts like a rotting onion. But as soon as you think you can handle it, it changes. It morphs like a crowded apartment building in which everyone is cooking something different, the smells tangling together to form something foul. Then it becomes heavy and smothering. The layers of rancid aromas explode like baby spiders from an egg sac, and they attack. A physical assault on the senses. The smell of death is unrelenting when unleashed.

One of her technicians is standing beside her, nervous and overly chatty.

"I know there are police everywhere, but I am still a little nervous. I have to be honest with you. This seems insane now that we are here. The bomb-sniffing dogs were dispatched, right?" she asks, speaking more loudly than she should.

"You have got to stop mentioning the police," Wren warns, keeping her voice at a low volume. "The whole point of this is to avoid pandemonium, not to incite it."

"I know. I'm sorry."

"You have to keep it together. Things may get intense, and I can't have you falling apart on me."

"Of course. No, I'm ready."

For a moment, Wren feels like maybe she has been too harsh.

"It's normal to feel nervous. I'm nervous too. But our job is to ignore that and get to the task at hand. Now, what do you smell?" Wren asks.

The young woman's nostrils flare, and her eyes widen.

"Is that?"

"Bingo," Wren replies.

"Shit."

"Don't panic. We have to be smart about this," Wren instructs. She locks eyes with Leroux across the thick sea of people. He is trying to appear casual but sticks out like a sore thumb in his neatly pressed suit. "Stay calm and follow me."

Together, Wren and the young technician cross the barrage of festivalgoers.

"What the hell are you eating?" A woman holding a plastic cup cranes her neck to look at the paper plate her companion is foraging through, and he shrugs his shoulders before pulling it away defensively.

"Some kind of bourbon chicken and rice. I don't know. Why?"

"Smells like hot garbage," she answers and wrinkles her nose.

"No, it doesn't smell like anything but bourbon sauce," he declares emphatically and shoves the plate under her nose as she prematurely recoils.

Wren passes by before hearing the women's response. The stench of human decomposition is starting to permeate the air, and people are taking notice. She drags her colleague past a man playing the trumpet. He blasts cheerful notes through the air like a fine mist. Several people around him have broken into dance. They pull and spin one another with that genuine kind of laughter that only comes with a truly carefree moment. But Wren knows that under the shiny exterior of this scene, there is rot. She blinks and pushes toward Leroux, stopping next to him and turning her head to the side to muffle their words.

"We are close. I'm sure you can smell it too."

She flicks her eyes to meet his, and he nods, scanning the crowd. They move together to follow the scent. The technician trails a bit behind as she pretends to scroll through her phone. Leroux's eyes are wild as he searches for the source. He usually rigidly regulates his emotional responses, and it is horrifying to see this crack in his armor. Wren takes a deep breath and wills her mind to focus.

"Your eyes look like they are going to fling themselves right out of your head. Chill," Wren offers to Leroux, shocked to find him looking at her with authority. She hides the desperation from her own face and tries again. "Look for flies."

"Flies at a nasty music festival, in the middle of the summer, in Louisiana. Got it."

"Do I need to give you a quick refresher on the tenacity and discipline of the blowfly?"

"Absolutely not. I got it. We're looking for a shit ton of flies."

She nods and returns her eyes to the crowd. She scans the herd quickly, trying to take note of everything that she can. They squeeze through a large congregation of revelers, approaching one of the smaller stages. It's small only in comparison to the massive main stage. The wood that holds it up, forming the foundation, is bent, scuffed, and faded from many summers baking in the sun. Now, a lively jazz ensemble sways and stomps on the stage's ancient floor, playing a buoyant tune. The music dances, teasing at a crescendo before finally swelling up in a chaotic wave of sound. The afternoon sunlight bounces off the instruments hoisted in the air, making the trumpets and saxophone shine like solid gold.

A thin black cloud emerges on the left side of the stage, toward the back. If she wasn't already so close to the metal barricade separating the crowd from the stage, she wouldn't have been able to see it, let alone hear it. The cloud buzzes like a field of wildflowers being pollinated. Except this is no pastoral field, and those aren't busy bees. These insects are looking for something far less sweet-smelling, preferring the foul bouquet of decaying flesh instead.

Without taking her eyes off the circling parade of flies making their way between the crumbling wooden slats, she grabs a handful of fabric from the side of Leroux's shirt and twists. He stops immediately.

"What is it?" he asks without looking at her.

"Beneath the stage, left side, toward the back."

He darts his eyes to the location and draws in a sharp breath. "Follow me."

He pushes sideways toward the end of the barricade. A security officer sits on a tall, wooden stool. He has one leg bent up on the rung beneath him and is absentmindedly bobbing his head to the music. Leroux approaches him and leans close to his ear.

"NOPD," he declares just above a whisper.

He opens his jacket to provide an inconspicuous visual of his badge. The security officer's eyes flit down to it, and he nods. Leroux peeks behind his own shoulder.

"We have to check out the stage area, but we don't need to have the entire crowd panicking. Can you help us with that, Officer . . . ?"

"Blum," the young officer finishes, clearing his throat and straightening up on the stool. He runs a hand over his stubble-covered jaw before resting it on his thigh. "No problem, detective. Come on through. I will stick around and try to keep everything calm."

Leroux claps a hand on his shoulder. "Thanks, we appreciate it. Come on, Muller."

He waves Wren and the technician through, and the three of them walk around the left side of the stage. The odor is unmistakable. As they near the flies, the air becomes thick and hazy. It's like walking into another realm, one filled with death and decay. Wren drops to a knee and peers between the slats where a portion of the wood has rotted away. It's dark under the stage. Her eyes adjust to the curtain of blackness, and a familiar form takes shape. Crumpled and motionless, laying almost directly in the center of the area beneath the stage, is the source of the blowflies' gathering. The smell is unbearable as she moves closer to it.

"Is there a way to get under the stage?" Wren straightens up, stifling a gag.

"There is a door back here."

Wren walks around to the back, where Leroux is already crouching low. His hand clicks open a latch. She removes the small flashlight from her back pocket and flicks it on. The beam of light casts forward and comes to a stop, bending itself around the motionless object. Illuminated in front of her is the distorted body of what appears to be a woman in her twenties. She is lying on her stomach with arms outstretched beneath her as if freefalling from a plane moments before the parachute opens. Wren quickly sees the mangled mess of flesh and bone where her right knee should be. She pans the light from legs to head, and her breath catches briefly as the victim's half-open eyes light up like a demon's. They stare directly back at Wren, staring but seeing nothing. Her face is filthy, painted with dirt, blood, and grime. Wren clicks the flashlight off and takes a moment to compose herself, crouched at the small door.

"It's what we thought, and it's bad," she says. She can hear him mutter "shit" under his breath. "Unfortunately, I'm going to need to get closer."

Leroux uses the back of his hand to wipe his forehead. "You're not seriously thinking about crawling under there, are you?"

"Not all the way in, but if I can just get a little closer, I'll be able to see exactly what we are working with. She looks like she has something in her right hand."

Wren makes her way to the end of the stage and stops to gently kick at the wood in front of her. It crumbles away, and she looks at Leroux.

"Found a weak spot," she reports.

He bends down next to her as she pulls away pieces of rotting wood. A small hole begins to form. Leroux peers into the darkness, using his phone to illuminate as far as he can.

"You sure about this, Muller?"

Wren nods and throws her hair into a messy bun on the top of her head. She reaches into her back pocket and brings out a pair of black nitrile gloves, snapping them onto her hands.

"Positive. Now watch my back."

She clicks on the flashlight and puts it between her lips as she dives headfirst into the blackness. The performance slams overhead as she slowly makes her way toward the body in front of her. The space is cramped and hot. There is only enough room for her to squat uncomfortably with her head bent at a sharp angle or crawl. She crawls forward and feels the ache of rocks and uneven ground rubbing against her knees. As she inches closer, the full savagery of this young woman's death is revealed. She has a number of cuts, bruises, and wounds covering her form, including a large laceration across her neck, her dark, curly hair matted to her face and neck with both fresh and old blood.

"Jesus."

The word almost falls out of Wren's mouth, muffled by the flashlight between her teeth. Leroux is waiting impatiently at the entrance. He squints at the carnage.

"I imagine it's bleak in there," he says with a sigh.

Wren shakes her head, turning it slightly to peek over her shoulder at him. "This is really vicious work, Leroux. The worst yet."

"Fuck. I feel like we are so close to nailing this bastard."

Wren looks back at the assaulted corpse in front of her and shifts her gaze to the woman's right hand, splayed outward to her side as if perpetually reaching for something just out of her grasp. The hand is curled around something, and Wren carefully begins peeling back each finger, forcing the stiffness to give way beneath her gloved hands. Her efforts unveil the unmistakable lines and symbols of a map. Wren spies marked plots and a key that labels the famous residents of notable tombs. This map is for St. Louis Cemetery No. 1.

"Someone got a bag out there?" Wren calls behind her and unfolds the map completely.

It's the kind of map they hand out to tourists once they show up for their guided tour of St Louis Cemetery No. 1, eager to gawk at and dissect the sights in front of them. This one is detailed to a point, even including the trees that separate the paths and alleyways that line the City of the Dead. Wren traces the pathways with her eyes, searching for something that doesn't belong, a sign to explain why this map found itself in the iron grip of a dead woman. In the cluster of gravesites toward the middle of the map, she spots a small crimson *X*, involuntarily gasping slightly at the discovery.

"What is it?" Leroux questions.

"There's a guide map of St. Louis Cemetery 1 down here with a spot marked off in red. I don't think this victim is the only present he left for us to find today."

"Shit. All right, come on out. Let's get her out of here and head over there. We have to contain this. Now."

Wren nods and bags the map, sealing it shut before taking one last look at the battered body before her. In her final, solemn gaze she notices something she hadn't before. On the victim's right wrist is a white smartwatch, a standout because of its pristine condition. It is brand-new and bears none of the wear of the rest of the victim's effects. There is no way that this watch was on that wrist before or at the time of death.

"Muller. Let's go!" Leroux trills impatiently. His eyes betray the thoughts racing around his head. She can see that he is already calculating their next moves. A true veteran of this world.

Wren sees the haze of doubt and frustration hanging over Leroux but doesn't let it impede her diligent tending to the crime scene in front of her.

"Yeah, John, I hear you. Just one second."

She reaches out a gloved hand to examine the watch and gently taps the screen to life. A cast of blue light floods the dark, cramped space. It asks for a numerical passcode.

"Hand me the map, Muller," Leroux barks. "Let's move!"

She ignores him and looks desperately around the space that felt so suffocating a moment ago, but now looks hollow and deep. She uses a hand to cast the flashlight's beam at the area around the body, hoping for more information, but sees only dirt, dust, and insects. She forces out a frustrated sigh and drops her eyes.

"Just thought I saw something," she squeaks.

She grips the evidence bag with the map securely inside and maneuvers her body toward the exit. Wren's eyes meet Leroux's, and she stretches her arm out to hand him the bag. She glances at the tiny crimson X for a beat longer.

"Read me the plot number where the red X is."

Leroux raises an eyebrow and is clearly exasperated.

"What?" he complains, but looks down at the map, smoothing the evidence bag out to see the numbers better. "The print is unbelievably tiny. One five oh . . . three. What is this all about?"

"One five oh three . . . one five oh three . . . one five oh three," Wren repeats to herself softly as she scoots her body back toward the dead woman's. With a gloved hand, she taps the watch, and it blinks back to life. She swipes, and it asks again for the four-digit passcode. Wren types the numbers, hesitating before hitting the final digit. Her breath hitches as she gives it a quick tap. The watch opens to reveal one application on the screen: the alarm.

"Wren!" Leroux's voice raises with a clear tone of frustration. Wren tries to calm her heartbeat thundering in her chest. "Are we leaving, or . . . ? Tell me before doing anything else!"

"I found something, John," she answers finally, looking behind her. "She has a brand-new smartwatch on her wrist that doesn't match the state of the rest of her. It was clearly placed on her postmortem. That plot number? One five oh three? Well, that is the watch's passcode, and I am now staring at the only open application. The alarm."

Wren pauses and sees Leroux's face drop. He rubs his eyes, handing the bag to another officer.

"How long?"

Wren looks at the alarm application. The only one on the screen is set for two p.m.

"Forty-five minutes from now."

"We gotta move. Landry, Cormier, and Fox, you're with Will. Go on ahead and clear the cemetery. I'll follow with Muller."

Flushed, he turns back to Wren.

"Get out of there. Let's go."

Wren crawls out toward the opening. She spots her technician hovering to the side and beckons to her.

"Call the office and get a couple of transporters out here," she instructs, and watches as the young woman immediately hits a button on her phone.

Wren haphazardly snaps the gloves off her hands and dusts her knees as she hastily follows Leroux through the crowd now forming along the cordoned-off perimeter. People's faces are twisted in fear, lurid curiosity, and confusion. They whisper to one another and crane their heads to try to catch a glimpse of the now conspicuous action. Lively music still blares from a farther stage, but the band directly ahead has cut its performance short. Wren hadn't even noticed until now.

CHAPTER 17

SEEING THE BULLET FROM HIS Glock hit its intended target feels satisfying in a way Jeremy can't describe. He could have hit Katie and Emily, too, with ease, but he isn't finished playing yet. It's a meal too delectable not to draw out, bite by bite.

He watches Katie and Emily running aimlessly through the verdant grounds. Jeremy keeps them in his sight and allows them to feel like they have created a safe distance between themselves and him. Katie is frantically wiping Matt's brain matter off her face and stumbles, falling behind. She is foolish, and Matt was practically a Neanderthal, but at least Emily is a fighter. She brings the challenge. He notices one of the flashlights flicker, dim, and go dark, as it bounces through the thick overgrowth.

Down to one light.

He smiles and picks up his pace a bit as "(Don't Fear) The Reaper" by Blue Oyster Cult begins to play, moving with the music. He is the Reaper tonight.

Katie is sobbing loudly across the tree line, and her voice reaches a pitch not unlike that of a rabbit suddenly confronting a bloodthirsty predator. Jeremy glances at his watch and allows a grin to slowly form across his face. It has been a few hours since he dropped his guests out here, and as he watches Katie takes a clumsy step, with her right leg lifted higher than a natural stride requires. The drugs are taking effect. He is starting to feel giddy at the realization that his experiment is working.

After reading about the Jamaican ginger poisonings during Prohibition, he felt inspired. In the Deep South during the early 1930s, some brilliant minds conjured a form of Jamaican ginger, or "jake" as it was better known, that was able to pass through the US Justice Department's rigid regulations. With the help of an unwitting MIT professor, they created a formula that used tricresyl phosphate because it was able to pass the tests without ruining the taste. This revolutionary bootlegger recipe ultimately resulted in a plethora of patrons walking with their legs stretched high and their toes unable to extend upward. The paralyzing epidemic that became known, somewhat dubiously, as "jake leg," and allowed researchers to determine too late that tricresyl phosphate is actually a dangerous neurotoxin that causes nerve cell death and damage to the myelin sheaths that aid in vital muscle movements. When ingested in substantial amounts, the chemical will cause gastrointestinal distress and partial paralysis in the limbs. And after daily injections of the chemical through her IV lines, Katie seems to be presenting with a rousing case of jake leg right on time.

Katie begins screaming to Emily that her leg is going numb, and Jeremy can see Emily desperately trying to convince her to push forward. He smiles as Katie withers down into a ball, pressing her knees into the swampy earth. He begins closing the gap between himself and them. He can see Emily weighing her options as she fearfully scans the tree line in front of them with their remaining light. Katie is sobbing and gagging, and Emily tries to hoist her to her feet with an arm around her waist.

Emily is ready to abandon her. Jeremy can feel it. Self-preservation will win. He pumps the shotgun once and places the scope to his eye. Emily and Katie hear the sound, and Emily tries again to pull Katie along. Jeremy squeezes the trigger and hits his target with ease. Katie lets out an agonized screech as the bullet rips through her right kneecap, leaving a mangled mess of flesh and muscle flayed in each direction on her leg. She crumbles beneath the weight of her upper body and hits the moist ground with a slapping sound.

Emily's choice is clear. She flees.

Jeremy slings the shotgun over his back and slides the bowie knife from its sheath as he swiftly walks toward Katie's pathetic sobs. Like an apparition, he appears in front of her, and her eyes are wild with fear. He grins and squats beside her, pushing a piece of matted hair behind her ear.

"Shhh," he whispers with a smile.

He grabs a handful of her hair, tilts her head back, and slowly drags the blade across her throat. He holds her there for a moment, allowing her to sputter and struggle until her body goes limp. Jeremy closes his eyes and listens to the music, both the organic symphony of the bayou and the canned music slithering through the speakers. He lets Katie's head drop into the mud and cracks his neck.

Now, where did Emily run off to?

CHAPTER 18

"This is Dr. Wren Muller from the ME's office. We need an ambulance to 425 Basin Street."

Wren digs through her bag, balancing her phone on her shoulder. The minutes are ticking by quickly as Leroux weaves the car through traffic toward their destination, toward a victim who might still be saved.

"Yes, St. Louis Cemetery 1. Possible medical emergency. If you can meet us at the entrance, we should be there in about"—she pauses to look at the dashboard clock—"eight minutes. Okay. Thank you."

She lets the phone drop to the seat next to her and snaps another pair of gloves onto her hands. Her face is an equal mix of calm and resolve. Pieces of her hair have fallen loose from the high bun on the crown of her head. They fall around her hairline and lay delicately across her cheeks, now sprinkled with dirt from the crime scene.

The New Orleans landscape speeds by as Leroux honks aggressively at the car in front of them. Anyone who fails to pull over at the sound of their sirens falls victim to an unrelenting slew of curse words. His knuckles are white as they grip the steering wheel. He's not your typical jaded detective from a big box office thriller.

"Do you think this is a trap, Muller?" he asks finally, his tone measured and deliberate.

Wren leans her elbow against the passenger-side window, resting her temple in her hand.

She sighs. "I have to believe it's not. And either way, we both have to treat it like it's not. But just remember that we are adequately prepared if the situation proves otherwise."

Leroux nods almost imperceptibly.

Wren straightens up. "Besides, Will and his gang of shiny youths will be there to back us up."

A small smirk plays at the corner of her lips, and Leroux lets out a little chuckle.

"Youths," he says, shaking his head. "Come on, they're rookies, but they have been outside the womb longer than that, Muller."

"I know. I'm only joking. If I didn't trust their abilities, I wouldn't be leaving my safety in their capable paws."

Leroux turns serious. "I just worry that this guy is going to be sitting close by, watching while we all run around a cemetery gobbling up his poisoned breadcrumbs."

Leroux turns right onto Basin Street. The corner is bustling with tourists and townies alike. A group of three women piles out of a massive yoga studio and toward a café with outdoor seating. People enjoy their lunch outside on this bright Louisiana afternoon, nibbling on buttery croissant sandwiches within sight of where someone might be desperately fighting to stay alive. He reaches the cemetery entrance, dotted with tall palm trees that mock the imposing white wall surrounding it. They bend slightly in the breeze and shake their fronds, welcoming visitors to this strange landmark, completely blind to the horrors that await inside.

Wren nods. "I know. The same scenario ran through my mind too. But our only choice is to try. I'm praying that the ambulance sees more action than I do this afternoon."

CHAPTER 19

EMILY'S FEET ALMOST HOVER ABOVE the ground as she glides over unfamiliar terrain, with only a bouncing beam of light to guide her way. She did exactly what Jeremy had hoped. She abandoned Katie and indulged her own primal urge to survive.

He can feel Emily's sudden, overwhelming panic. She pushes forward, but the swampy ground swallows her every step, making a sickening sound and forcing her to exert more energy than she can sustain. The bayou is working in tandem with Jeremy, lending its hand to help him accomplish his final vision. The environment belongs to him. And, more important, it has turned against her.

She stops, pushing her back into the hollow of a tree. Crumbs of earth and frenzied insects cascade down her shoulders as she leans against the moss and the mud of the massive trunk. He wonders if she thinks she is being quiet. He can hear her breath, quick and shallow. He tastes the fear in the air and can't contain himself any longer.

"Emily!" his voice booms through the chaos. "It's Cal, Emily!"

She cringes and tries to keep the sob from escaping her throat. He hears it tumble out in a choked whimper.

"It appears that you are my final girl," he yells with a chuckle. "Have you located the perimeter yet?"

She can hear him coming closer. He is intentionally making himself known as she shuffles through the underbrush. This is his crescendo.

"Do you even know what direction you are running toward?" he laughs. "Well, don't let me discourage you. Run, rabbit, run!"

In an unplanned show of theater, he shoots his handgun into the air, and Emily instinctively takes off. She runs through a stream, splashing loudly and allowing the thick mud to swallow her shoes whole. She leaves them behind as she bounds out of the water and through a wall of thicket. The sharp spines pierce and rip at her legs, arms, and face, but she keeps moving. He is running now, too, gaining on her. She serpentines to avoid a fate like Matt's or Katie's.

Suddenly, it appears. Like an oasis in the desert, she sees the perimeter. A metal fence that runs through the trees and clearly delineates Jeremy's kingdom from freedom. It's only about six feet tall, and all she needs is momentum to clear it. She stops briefly and then dashes forward, diving onto the fence, hooking the toes on her right foot and the fingers on her right hand onto the links.

All at once, searing pain. A jolt of electricity takes hold of every cell as her body stiffens and convulses before being tossed back into the nightmare behind her.

"I am a little offended that you didn't think I would electrify my perimeter fence," Jeremy condescends as he steps over a fallen tree and hovers over her.

She sputters out blood and furiously oscillates between blacking out and keen focus. She rolls onto her side and begins to crawl. She desperately claws at the mud and moss, propelling herself forward as best she can. She doesn't have a plan. Her only thought is to place as much distance as possible between herself and the monster behind her. Jeremy slowly follows, slipping the bowie knife from its sheath and kneeling to loop his arm around her throat, pulling her up on her knees.

Before saying another word, he uses his forefinger and thumb to open her right eye wide as she struggles against him. He allows a couple of drops of tropicamide to hit her eyeball, and before she can register her blurred vision, he does the same to the left, keeping her still in a choke hold.

"Stop! What is that?" she yells, pulling her head back.

"Tropicamide eye drops," he responds flatly, making sure to add a little extra to each eye. "Ever had an eye exam, Emily? Experienced blurred vision for several hours and been told to please not operate heavy machinery?"

He smiles, knowing she can still make out his expressions, though not clearly. She blinks rapidly to try to clear her vision to no avail.

"You ever hear the phrase 'C5, stay alive'?" He looks into her eyes as she stares back at him.

"Just let me go, please. I won't tell anyone if you just let me go," Emily pleads.

The survival instinct that got her here has moved into the bargaining stage. Jeremy leans his forehead into hers, so they are touching.

"Don't interrupt." He winks and pulls his head back. "You see, if you sever the spinal cord above the C5 cervical vertebrae, then you will most certainly kill the person attached to it. Why is that?"

He mindlessly flicks a bug from Emily's shoulder and waits for a response.

"Just stop. Please stop!"

His face twists into a look of disgust. "Nothing? A second-year medical student, and you can't answer my basic anatomy question?"

Emily closes her eyes. "Please," she whispers.

He ignores her pleas and continues, "The C1 and C4 vertebrae flank the nerves responsible for letting your diaphragm know how to breathe." He points the tip of the bowie knife at her diaphragm as he says this. "If you sever that particular part of the spinal cord, then you will asphyxiate, and you will die. C4, breathe no more."

"Why are you telling me this?" She is panicking now.

"I'm not going to do that to you, Emily. Relax," he continues. "What do you think? That I'm a monster?"

He gets close to her face again and then looks at the knife, twisting it in his hand. She watches, too, as the small amount of light that has crept in from the moon bounces off the blade. Again, the bayou has bent to his will. It has given him a spotlight for his show. A sharp pain shoots through her lower back. The red-hot sensation is all she can feel, and she realizes too late that he has plunged the bowie knife into her back.

"If you sever the spinal cord anywhere below C5, you'll likely stay alive. But you will also most definitely suffer paralysis in the portion of the body below that vertebra," he continues and pats Emily's leg. "I chose the lumbar region."

She grabs Jeremy's shirt with her hand, twisting the black fabric with her fist and looking around wildly.

"It's a fucked-up little rhyme, huh?" He grins again and pulls the blade out in one swift motion.

CHAPTER 20

S T. LOUIS CEMETERY No. 1 looms on the left. Dark secrets of the past contained within its white walls are
newly invigorated with this present horror. Wren imagines
rows of the dead watching this monster at work. He's made
each of them an involuntary witness to his crimes inside of
this sacred city.

The sound of an ambulance echoes through the street noise
as it approaches. Leroux pulls the car behind Will's. Without
speaking, he and Wren step out into the thick air. The officers
at the scene appear around the corner, looking serious and
already glistening with sweat.

"Perimeter looks clear. Gates are secured. Landry and
Knox are inside, clearing the way toward plot 1503."

Will looks more serious than ever, and Wren knows why.

"You haven't heard anything?" she asks.

He shakes his head and squints in the sunlight. "Nothing."

The ambulance pulls in, silencing its sirens. Two paramedics jump out and grab kits from a small compartment on the side of the truck.

"Escort these guys behind us, will you?" Leroux gestures to the man and woman who just exited the ambulance. Will nods and retreats to fill them in before following behind Leroux and Wren.

The oldest burial ground in New Orleans stretches for what feels like an eternity ahead of them. The winding passages can play tricks on the mind. It's eerily silent. This place acts as a vacuum. Even with the bustling city outside the walls, Wren strains to make out a sound, any sign of life. Static answers back. The dead keep their secrets.

Turning right, they make their way to the plots of underground burials. Everything is still. Even the large crow that has landed on a nearby tomb is uncharacteristically silent. He looks to them and sways slightly on the crumbling stone beneath his clawed feet. Wren wonders if he has come to watch this reveal.

"Shovels! We need shovels!" Wren shouts as she spots the freshly dug grave in an otherwise defunct part of the cemetery.

Leroux impulsively runs forward toward the upturned earth, spotting something else. Officers rush to cover the surrounding area. Guns drawn, they prowl and search for any waiting trap. Ignoring Leroux's discovery, Wren rushes to the groundskeeper shed behind them. It's locked, as expected, but a shovel leans conveniently against the small structure. She grabs it and runs back to the site where Leroux thrusts the object he saw in Wren's face. It ticks loudly at her.

"An egg timer," he says breathlessly. "It matches the alarm back at the other scene. We have almost exactly twenty minutes." He is flushed and sweating.

"If someone is in there, that isn't good. No way they'd be conscious under there," she worries, slitting her eyes at the mound of fresh earth before them. "We have to dig. Now."

Leroux quickly shrugs off his jacket, letting it fall to the ground, and pushes up his sleeves.

"You use the shovel," he commands and kneels to start scooping loose soil, using his hands and arms as a crude shovel.

Wren digs furiously. She throws soil aside with abandon as more officers join in their efforts. They are silent workers. No one speaks. The only sound is the shovel hitting earth and collective heavy breathing. Wren's hopes have shattered, but she tries to hide it from her teammates. She had hoped they would find someone out in the open or even in an aboveground tomb. Someone buried alive has very little time for survival, and forty-five minutes is a big stretch, no matter how healthy the victim is. They have no idea what this type of container this person was buried in, how deep it lies, and or how long they've been in there. They don't even know if someone is in there or not. Despite all of this, Wren digs at a breakneck pace. Her hope shattered, yes, but not beyond repair.

Leroux eagerly takes the shovel from Wren's hands, plunging it into the dirt as hard and fast as he can. The seconds tick away loudly on the old egg timer, and he can see on Wren's face that every second counts. It feels like they have been digging for days. They've dug close to three feet down already. Leroux wipes the back of his arm across his forehead, smearing dirt along the sweat.

"Guys, what if it is a full six feet down?" an officer asks hesitantly.

Wren shakes her head and blows out some air. "Then we dig six feet."

Leroux keeps going like a machine. He doesn't respond to his colleagues' concerns, but he feels them. Six feet of earth is an enormous amount to clear straight down without prior planning, proper tools, or decent hydration and rest. He hadn't even noticed until now that the two paramedics on the scene have taken off their uniform shirts to scoop dirt alongside them. He catches the eye of a medic and nods a silent message of appreciation. She nods back and continues to pull dirt from the grave site.

They work together like a well-oiled machine. Dirt flies in all directions. All parts of this team are laser-focused. Leroux steals a glance at the timer, and the tip of the spade hits something solid. He slams it down again to make sure. Metal on wood. He glances again at the time. Four minutes left.

"We hit something!" he yells, moving a bit to the side to clear more dirt away from the wooden casket slowly becoming unearthed in the soil.

Wren scrapes her shovel head across the top of the casket to clear the dirt away, and others gather to scoop the bulk away from the end. The grave was loosely dug. He wanted them to find and open it, but he also wanted them to struggle a little first. Anticipation permeates the air as a handle on the end of the coffin is exposed.

"Let's try to pull it from one end," Will suggests, gesturing toward the exposed handle. "We can try to tip it to get the lid off without dumping more dirt inside."

Wren nods. "You three pull up, and we will guide you from this end. When I say stop, stop. I don't want you to tip it too vertical."

They nod and grab the handle tight. They place their free hands on the sides of the casket to steady themselves. The officers pull forcefully while Wren and the paramedics push from the other end. With a great creaking sound, the casket frees itself from the surrounding earth.

"Stop!" Wren yells and puts her hand up.

They pause and gingerly release their grip on the end, leaving it propped up on the heap of displaced dirt beside it. Wren starts prying the lid and Leroux rushes to help. It comes free after a quick jerk from both of them, and they raise the lid to the waiting hands above.

Time stands still. The slow tick of the timer is the only thing that cuts through the silence.

"Oh god!" a paramedic exclaims, clapping his hand over his mouth in horror.

The woman inside the coffin looks to be in her late twenties. She has auburn hair, matted with mud, fanned out around her head. Her eyes are closed. Her face is peaceful though coated in grime. Dried vomit clings to her cheek and the lining of the coffin. Her feet are bare. They are scraped raw and crusted with dried blood and soil. Her white T-shirt shows ample signs of wear. A deeply set stain creeps down her left side and around her back. The officers know without Wren's help that it's blood. A lot of blood. The woman in the coffin is still, and she's silent.

The timer goes off.

CHAPTER 21

JEREMY OPENS HIS EYES, FEELING rested even though he's only had two hours of sleep. He sits up in bed, peeking behind the shades in his room, letting the warm light dribble in to greet him. His eyes sweep over the wide expanse of trees and green that stretch out in front of him like an ocean. It's his own version of Aokigahara, the so-called Suicide Forest, in Japan, where lost souls go to die.

He left Emily in that forest last night, paralyzed from the waist down with nowhere to go. After he pulled the knife from her back, her eyes went wild. They bored into his own and almost pulsated with shock. He crouched there for a moment next to her, just watching as she gasped in pain. In her delirium, she even grasped for him like a lifeline.

When he at last left her in the cold blanket of darkness, she had called out to him. She had called for "Cal" to come back. She had begged him not to leave her there alone. Her wails had been his lullaby for a deep, if brief, sleep.

Now, he pulls on a clean shirt. It's white and crisp. He stops to brush his teeth and carefully coifs his blond hair into place. As he makes his way out back, he listens to the sound the wooden planks make beneath his feet. His black boots pound heavily against them. He wonders then if she can hear him approaching. Did sleep find her exhausted, terrorized body at all?

"Emily!" he calls out into the distance.

He waits for a sound. Nothing but cicadas and birds answer him.

"You're not dead, are you?" he yells again, only half joking. The only thing to answer him is his beloved bayou.

He picks up his pace, entering the dense trees and stepping off the wooden boardwalk toward the perimeter fence where he left her body. He's anxious and excited.

"Emily, I hope you can forgive me," he chirps, stifling a giggle.

He enters the open space near the fence and spots her. She's leaning, almost completely horizontal, with her back against the fence. The wire fencing bends behind her, allowing a gaping hole to form. She's motionless. For a moment, he wonders if she is dead.

No. No, that won't do.

He picks up his pace, striding toward her with searching eyes. She can't be dead yet. His entire plan would be ruined. She is supposed to be his message. She's supposed to be his warning.

As he comes to her still form, he squints his eyes. Crouching down, he can see plainly it's not Emily who lays before him. It's Katie.

His heart quickens in his chest as he puts it together in his mind.

He missed.

He must have missed her spinal cord somehow. She was clearly still able to move when he left her last night. His mind races, as he places his arm through the hole. Emily bested him. She dragged Katie across the property and used her body to absorb the fence's electric pulses. He touches the blood smeared onto the wire above Katie. Emily let Katie become a conduit and crawled over her to escape. The electric pulses would have barely affected her through Katie, if at all.

He stands, gazing out into the tall grass and expanse of trees outside the perimeter of his man-made arena. Emily is gone. As he closes his own eyes to the morning sun, he is at least thankful that he was overprepared. She won't get far with her wounds and even if she does, still can't see past her own blurred nose thanks to the tropicamide. He'll be able to catch up to her soon enough. But this thought offers no relief. Everything has changed.

CHAPTER 22

WREN ALLOWS HERSELF ONLY A moment. Then she gets to work, reaching out her gloved hand for a pulse. She closes her own eyes and focuses on palpating for this woman's carotid artery. She presses lightly into it and desperately tries to sense any kind of life. She feels it then, the slightest movement in the victim's cardiac cycle beneath her fingertips.

Wren's world brightens to vivid Technicolor. She looks up at the paramedics with wild eyes, yelling, "You're up! She has a pulse!"

The two medics spring into action. They roll the victim slightly onto her side and discover the source of the dark blood staining her shirt behind her hip.

"There's a wound to her cervical spine," the medic reports, snapped out of his initial shock and regaining focus and professionalism. "Though it appears that it's um . . . been tended to."

Wren leans forward incredulously. "What?"

She peers at the bloodied bandages over the wound in this woman's upper back.

"He bandaged her wounds?" Wren questions, brow knitted into a look of pure confusion. "He's never done that before. Actually, I can't think of any killer who has ever done that before."

Leroux is shaking his head, trying to turn off the kitchen timer still blaring in his hands. An officer beside him takes it silently and clicks it off. Farther off, another officer is barking orders at the others to cordon off the scene and call for backup on the site.

"Let's get her out of here. We have to get her stable before anything else," a medic instructs.

With some help from Wren, they slide the woman from the coffin. They have already begun attaching various life-saving equipment to her, years of training making for seamless execution. Wren takes a moment to look back into the casket and inhales a sharp breath as she notices a full human skeleton crumbled to the side of it. The victim had been interred with the casket's original inhabitant. It's hard to say right now whether she was conscious when she entered this coffin. Wren doesn't ruminate on the nightmare of being buried alive for long. Leroux nudges her shoulder, and she is jolted from her thoughts.

"Look at the lid," he says rigidly, looking directly into her eyes as he does.

Wren's worst fears are confirmed as she sees lines of scratch marks chaotically crisscrossing the ancient wood. It looks like something out of a horror movie. Like *The Silence of the*

Lambs. The broken fingernail embedded in the stone of the infamous pit Buffalo Bill used to store his victims is forever ingrained in Wren's memory, and now she's confronted with a similar reality off-screen. Some of the marks have traces of blood smeared across them, and a quick look at the victim's hands shows that she had used them to claw and scratch until they bled. At some point in her entombment, she was conscious enough to realize where she was. She had spent who knows how long trying in vain to scratch through the wooden lid that closed in on her, perhaps not even knowing about the three feet of earth waiting for her on the other side.

"She's alive, John," Wren says finally, though finding herself unable to look away from the scratch marks. "She's got a pulse, and she'll know who this guy is. That's what matters."

Leroux loosens his tie. His jaw clenches, and the desperate hope in his eyes from moments earlier is long gone, replaced by a shattering flash of defeat.

"Did you see what I saw, Muller? She might as well be dead. I wouldn't be surprised if she ends up on one of your gurneys later tonight," he spits and turns around to half-heartedly toss a clod of dirt to the ground. "He fucking played us, and we fell for it."

Wren doesn't disagree. She felt the pulse with her own hand, and it was weak at best. There is little chance that the victim's brain is going to be able to recall anything with full clarity if she wakes up. But Wren doesn't say that. "You're wrong. He didn't play us."

Leroux turns quickly to face her. "How can you even bull-shit me right now, Muller? He didn't play us? We look like fools, racing against some clock that he laid out for us to find. That's exactly what he wanted."

His voice takes an aggressive tone Wren has never heard before. She isn't scared of him, but she is scared *for* him. She takes a slow, deep breath and then responds.

"No, John. He meant for her to be dead. He meant for us to be filled with false hope, prying this lid open with time to spare only to find a dead girl inside. That's what he planned, and it didn't happen." Leroux softens, and she continues, "We opened that lid, and we found a living human being inside. Someone who saw him, heard him, and, hell, probably smelled him. And even if she can't point us in the right direction when she wakes up, we'll still have saved her. A person. He failed. No matter what happens next, he already failed."

Wren climbs out of the hole they've both been standing in and bends over to dust the dirt from her pants. Leroux tilts his head back and groans, his old self again. He stands and follows Wren to the entrance. They match strides, both ragged and weary from their lifesaving efforts. More hair has escaped Wren's bun than is still contained by it. Her skin is flushed and painted with a sweat-soil paste. Leroux's hair is unruly and damp. Sweat has soaked through his dress shirt. They both try to believe the day's efforts were worth something as they walk away from this moment.

"The idea that he meant for this to go down differently. That he didn't get his moment, that's nice," Leroux concedes. "But it's like a participation trophy. I can put it on my shelf and it's an ego boost in the moment, but it's nothing like the real thing. A *real* win. We're no closer to nailing him. Any further loss of innocent life is on my hands."

PART

TWO

CHAPTER 23

J EREMY LEANS AGAINST A NEARBY tomb. It is humid this morning, and he uses his forearm to wipe beads of perspiration from his forehead as he lets his head fall back to look up at the clear expanse of the sky above. The St. Louis Cemetery is silent, even when full of tourists. Now, almost a full day after they dug up his victim and branded him a failure, this place somehow feels even more isolated from the world of the living.

New Orleans burials have always been steeped in lore. The city's unfortunate placement on a water table makes the ground one of the most inhospitable places for a freshly dead body. Caskets buried underground fill with water and eventually push themselves to the surface with even the slightest flooding. Attempts by early gravediggers to weigh the dead down almost always succumbed to rising water pressure eventually. When the caskets began floating down the New Orleans streets, it became clear that there was a need for a new solution. Now, the dearly departed are laid to rest above the ground. The labyrinthian constellation of tombs create an eerie atmosphere, earning it the moniker the City of the Dead. Fittingly, famed voodoo queen Marie Laveau calls this place home. Visitors have spent years marking the stone that surrounds her body with three *X*s in the hope that she will make their most unattainable dreams come true.

Now they don't allow just anyone into this burial ground. The Archdiocese of New Orleans created strict rules after vandals took to the crumbling tombs. These decaying graves are beautiful in their own way, but shining a light into one of them can put a macabre peep show on full display, with disarticulated skeletons scantily covered by remnants of fabric from eras long past. The city rushed to protect the sanctity of the dead.

Yet Jeremy entered this forbidden world by simply jumping the fence.

He remembers how, the last time he was here at this hour, he had to break the security camera pointed in this direction before dragging his victim through the gate, working fast to get her into the ground. He had done his research. He knew this spot was the site of an old, belowground burial, and once safely inside of the cemetery walls, dug the shallow grave in the moist earth easily. He remembers prying open the lid of the decrepit, splintering vessel and moving the disintegrated bones to one side of the casket to place his fresh addition inside. But most of all he remembers the delicious feeling of carefully taking a bracelet out of his pocket, small and fragile-looking, and slipping it onto the woman's left wrist before interring her in the stolen grave.

Jeremy remembers the old cliché about killers returning to the scenes of their crimes and finds a small bit of humor in it despite the disappointment of the last hours. He'd much rather be a walking cliché here, in the grotesque and stately beauty of the cemetery, than ever return to the venue of the jazz festival.

He thinks back to the swirl of people who raucously drank, ate, and laughed around him. How the air was heavy and thick, but with a slight breeze that drew even the most heat-sensitive away from the synthetic comfort of their air conditioners for the afternoon. He had felt secure and confident as the sickly-sweet smell of putrefying flesh mixed with the rank smells of carnival food. He remembers the pleasure of seeing the realization on a few faces in the crowd, the pungent aroma of two-day-old decomp overwhelming the more pleasant aroma of sugar-dusted beignets and the world's finest gumbo. They couldn't see her just then, but her smell betrayed her hiding place. She reached out from under that stage—an enduring vexation even after her screams were silenced. The anticipation was intoxicating.

Jeremy closes his eyes, and he can see her. He sees her wide, terrified eyes, her last bit of hope snuffed out in that dark bayou. Now those eyes have had the light drained from them, their heavy-hooded lids hanging low in a sleepy half stare. The thin, tight line that stretched across her lips, now a slack and lazy one. It's like she wants to say something but can't. The voices of dead are forever silenced. They're shells of clinically relevant tissue with no method of communicating what they truly experienced before ending up in a crime scene or on an autopsy table. No one can know the utter loneliness that precedes death until it comes for them. Physiologically, they can accurately explain what happens when a heart stops beating, but not the anguish that pours from someone's soul the moment they realize their life is being snuffed out by another.

Pacing the rows of the empty cemetery, Jeremy holds tight to these memories to ground himself in the wake of everything that's gone awry since he first laid out his careful plans. He reminds himself of his larger mission, the one he started almost seven years ago, and one he won't lose sight of again. There can be no more mistakes.

CHAPTER 24

THE CALL CAME MERE HOURS after they left the hospital. The victim went into respiratory distress and eventually suffocated. The doctors and nurses on call had attempted lifesaving ventilation procedures, but her body simply gave out. Her death report revealed that a stab wound severed the spinal roots in her C6 spinal region. She had been paralyzed from the waist down. Wren instinctively shook her leg when she learned this information.

The doctors also reported that the killer had tended to the wound he created, as Wren had already suspected. The blood loss was not as significant as it would have been if left untreated, making it unlikely as the final cause of death. The blood test results provided an even clearer picture of the victim's fate. Her system showed moderate quantities of poison hemlock, likely administered intravenously before she was placed into her living tomb. The hemlock finished the job that her killer had started. Wren had lingered on this detail when she first read it. It is a literary poison, and she wondered what it said about the killer who wielded it in this way.

With the body now lying lifeless and cold on her table in the autopsy suite, Wren can't help but think of the parents' faces at the hospital. Their tear-stained cheeks and their tired eyes burned in her memory. She can't even imagine the grief they'll feel when they discover the extent of the horror their daughter endured, what she saw and felt and suffered through. This killer's crimes are like an airborne virus, infecting everyone along the way to its primary target. It's all collateral damage to him, but to the real people involved, it consumes their every cell. For just a moment they had their daughter back and alive, only to have their hopes dashed. Though sometimes death is the only real mercy.

Wren dumps out the green bag with the victim's effects, transferred over to the medical examiner's office from the hospital where she took her last strained breaths hours earlier. The contents spill onto the steel table beside her body. There aren't many things inside of it. Her dirty, stained clothing was cut off her body while the doctors attempted to save her life at the ER. The back of her shredded white T-shirt is brown with old blood. There is dried vomit on her right sleeve, likely having dripped onto it after she lost consciousness. Her jeans are caked with mud. Wren is determined to figure out precisely what was done to this woman before her untimely death, but at the same time is terrified to discover the truth. She knows that this woman's last lucid hours must have been full of things even horror movie directors can't fathom.

Wren casts aside the clothing and returns to the bag's emptied contents. There is only one thing left. The only other possession the victim was transported with is a bracelet that, according to the accompanying report, was taken off her left wrist. Wren's eyes lock on this piece of jewelry. The bracelet is delicate and has a dangling silver anatomical heart charm with a small engraved E on its side. Her pupils focus and refocus, as if in disbelief. With her gloved hand, she touches it. She is looking to prove that it's really there, in the room with her, and half expects her fingers to pass through it. Instead, they connect with the cool metal, first the charm and then the rest of its length. It's real, and it's here.

Her thoughts are chaotic. They speed through her brain in undecipherable patterns. She imagines the inside of her mind sounds like a scratched CD skipping endlessly. She knows this bracelet. It belonged to her in another life. Now she stands in the place where she usually feels her most competent and strong, light-years away from the version of herself that once wore this bracelet, holding it again in her hands.

This bracelet belongs to Emily Maloney.

This bracelet belongs to Wren Muller.

CHAPTER 25

Jeremy can't help but think about how his grand return has gotten off to such a rocky start. Seven years. Seven years of plans and work has led up to this unsatisfactory showing. He watched the disaster unfold from what should have been a pleasurable vantage point yesterday, forced to remain hidden on the outside of the cemetery observing helplessly as his plan broke apart. Failure is never an easy pill to swallow, but for Jeremy it is like ingesting broken glass. He successfully evaded it for most of his life, yet somehow he's now awash in it.

He had planned it out so carefully, choosing victims and methods of murder that would trigger specific memories for people who had been working his case since the beginning. He had left clues, not all of which were subtle. The pages of "The Most Dangerous Game" he had shoved down that one woman's throat were almost comical in their obviousness. It was perhaps hubris to display his power over these frantic little creatures trying to catch him, but he was committed to calling out to Emily. He wanted to remind her of her former life, her real life. He could almost feel her return to that place in her mind where she was still a scared little rabbit running from him in a dark swamp.

After all these years, it is her escape that echoes most loudly in his mind. Walking into his arena that morning seven years ago and seeing Emily's escape route stretch out in front of him was excruciating—not in the least because he had to immediately dispose of Matt's and Katie's bodies and get to work on covering up any traces of his experiment. He had lived in that failure for years, perfecting his work and making sure not only that he would never feel that way again, but also that she wouldn't breathe her last breath without him finally being the one to snatch it from her. Her death is his to orchestrate.

Now, watching another meticulously planned moment shatter to pieces, he is seething. He pulled the strings too hard on his puppet show. He could feel them fraying from the pressure and snapping to reveal the man behind the curtain. The scene had been almost perfect, almost the show he had intended to create.

It can still be salvaged, and there is work to be done, but now all he can hear is the fresh memory of the satisfying sounds of shovels diving into the earth over and over again. The breaths, labored and fast. The group inside the blue tarps grunting and puffing out air. The officer and paramedics were filthy with cemetery dirt, all using their arms and hands to scoop the soil away before a man in his seventies politely pushed his way to the front of the crowd holding two spades in his grip. Jeremy can't remember ever seeing such a rare display of true kindness before or since, but despite this un-foreseen civilian aid, he had been confident in their imminent devastation.

Admittedly, it had been risky. Something of this magni-tude required a leap of faith, but he had leapt, nonetheless. His bells had chimed, and he had found their emphatic sound eu-phoric, blasting through the silence like an inappropriate joke. Crude and imposing. Jeremy had turned to face the street and leaned his back against the cemetery wall like a satisfied lover.

But, of course, everything that followed eclipsed any satis-faction he had previously enjoyed.

"You're up! She has a pulse!"

The words haunt him now. Even a day later, he can hear her say them again and again, her tone dripping with impe-riousness. She had loaded these words from her quiver and launched them from a tautly pulled bowstring with the force of a seasoned archer. They impale him even now.

At first, Jeremy had panicked at the thought that his unex-pectedly surviving victim had seen his face, that she knew his name and even his alias. But he had quickly comforted him-self in the knowledge that even if she had somehow survived paralysis and severe oxygen deprivation, she wouldn't have been mentally sound enough to put him in any real danger. The muscle spasms and almost constant seizures suffered in that tiny box would have caused lasting neurological damage. Her brain destroyed.

And beyond that, Jeremy knew from the start how rare it is for a plan to follow the initial blueprint without even minor deviations. Contingencies are built into plans for this exact reason, and Jeremy felt thankful for the hemlock he injected into his victim's sleeping body before placing her into that not-so-final resting place. Of course, it would have been better if she was found already dead upon exhumation, but contingency plans are better than abject failures. The poison hemlock coursed through her veins, and respiratory failure finished the job.

Just like Socrates.

He was seventy years old at the time of his trial for impiety and the corruption of youth. When found guilty of both charges by a jury of his peers, he was told he would be acting as his own executioner. Ancient Greece was nothing if not theatrical. Socrates was hastily led down to a jail cell and handed a cup of poison hemlock tea. He was instructed to drink and then walk around until he felt his legs give out beneath him. History would have us believe that his was a harmonious death. That he did as he was told and that he did so stoically. But Jeremy knows the real havoc that poison hemlock can wreak—vomiting, seizures, respiratory failure—and he is glad to see history repeat itself in his latest victim.

Jeremy knows it's not healthy to ruminate on his past failures. He can feel himself getting increasingly obsessive to the point of carelessness, but much like a plane in a nosedive toward the ground, he just can't stop himself.

CHAPTER 26

WRENS ARE TRULY MAGNIFICENT LITTLE creatures. They signify rebirth and protection, immortality, and strength. Because of the wren's small stature, most larger birds and predators underestimate its incredible ingenuity and intelligence. But while technically fragile, the wren outwits its underprepared predator to come out on top when threatened.

It's for all these reasons that she chose the name for herself.

Seven years ago, Wren Muller was Emily Maloney, working steadily toward her dream of becoming a doctor. She was trusting, naïve, and blissfully unaware of the horrors that would soon befall her. A perfect mark. And then, she was drugged, kidnapped, hunted, stabbed, and left for dead in a remote bayou—one that she still can't quite pin down on a map—by a sadistic killer masquerading as her lab partner and friend.

At first, she had blamed herself for missing the signs. She ran through it over and over in her mind. How she waited for what felt like hours on the ground with her eyes blurry and burning. How her back throbbed and her head pounded. How she didn't dare move for fear he would come back. She remembers the fear bubbling in her throat like bile, so all-encompassing that she thought she might drown in it. But, eventually, it faded. The torture he inflicted on her mind and body healed. She learned to survive, and, ultimately, to move on.

But now Cal's crooked smile haunts her once more.

She's transported back in time to that same cursed stretch of bayou and watches herself, bloody and bruised, feel behind her body to touch the deep wound in her lower back. He had missed the mark. Missed the spinal cord, wounding but not paralyzing her as he had intended. They were only second-year medical students together, after all. She remembers dragging Katie's body along the spongy ground. Her eyelids were like sandpaper that night, but her adrenaline carried her through the suffocating pain and exhaustion. She knew she had to redirect the electric current from the fence so she could pass it freely. It took every ounce of her strength to push Katie's limp body into it. She can't remember now what it felt like to climb over Katie's body, and she silently thanks her brain for protecting itself against the full extent of the sensory memory. She does, however, remember running. She ran for miles. It was like running through water.

She blinks herself from her racing memories and swallows hard.

Now she knows Cal was the Bayou Butcher. He had killed several women and men before her and is doing it again. She quickly snaps her glove from her right hand and snatches her cell phone.

"John." She says his name as a sob catches in her throat. "Are you on your way here?"

She can hear passing vehicles in the background.

"Yeah, I should be there in about five minutes. What's going on?"

She can hear the concern in his voice. She wants to scream at him that she knows who the Bayou Butcher is, that she has proof that he's back. She takes an unsteady breath in and glances at the bracelet.

"I'm okay. It's just when you get here, I have to drop some information on you. It's pretty big. Just don't want to blindside you." She's speaking too quickly, but she can't slow herself down, still reeling from this shotgun blast of reality.

"Stay put. I'm coming," he says kindly, but with his trademark steeliness.

The line cuts, and Wren drops her phone on top of the steel table in front of her. For a moment, she listens to her own breaths in the silent autopsy suite. After a minute, she grabs a scalpel handle. She carefully unwraps a blade and presses it to the handle until it clicks into place.

"I didn't finish the external exam," she says out loud as if talking to the victim herself.

She places the scalpel onto the sheet that covers the victim's torso, then replaces her gloves and straps a face shield around her head. She pulls down the sheet and holds the blade over the right shoulder, preparing to begin the Y-incision. Before the blade hits pallid flesh, Wren stops.

"I won't fail you, Emma," she promises, using the victim's name to punctuate her point. She can still hear Emma's parents' agonized voices saying the name to her in the hospital morgue as they cradled her lifeless hands in their own. "Take care of my Emma," her mother had pleaded.

Now, Wren squeezes her eyes shut like pressing a reset button. "I'm here to listen."

Tears threaten to form behind her eyes, but she stifles them with a hard blink. An external examination is not something you can just half-ass as a medical examiner or coroner. It's vital to the process. Once the first cut is made, everything changes. Wren refuses to allow her personal stake in this case to jeopardize the task ahead. This is Emma's time to speak, not Wren's time to grieve.

She begins at Emma's head, using her gloved hand to gently brush the matted hair off her forehead. Her eyes are only half open, making her look like someone about to fall asleep. Despite her heavy lids, it's clear to Wren that these eyes were once brilliantly blue. Unforgettable. Now, they are cloudy and dull. A pale haze has crept across the surface, making them look ghostly. It's an unfortunate side effect of death, but always harder to accept in a pair of eyes like these. She lifts a lid slightly to check for signs of petechial hemorrhaging. She detects no sign of the tiny blood vessels that burst in and around the eyes when a victim suffers from strangulation.

She can feel her heart race at the thought, and her hands begin to tremble. She gives in for only a second to the lump that has been sitting in her throat. Sometimes just vocalizing a sob can make the pressure dissipate, but instead she straightens back up. She shakes it off and brings her hands down to the next area for examination.

The intubation tube is still taped to Emma's face. Wren inspects it before slowly pulling it out of her throat. As she tugs on the tube, she gingerly removes the tape that keeps it in place. Trapped air rushes out of Emma's mouth, creating a slight breathy sound—easily mistakable as a sign of life to the untrained ear. She pauses for a moment, remembering the scene in *The Silence of the Lambs* when the forensic pathologist removes a death's-head moth's cocoon from the throat of one of Buffalo Bill's victims. Wren always shivered when the trapped air escaped as he pulled it out and credits the scene with helping shape her early fascination with the human body and what happens to it after death.

Emma's arms have minor bruises scattered across them, no doubt the result of her trying to escape the underground prison after being entombed. These wounds don't correlate to beatings of any kind. Wren notes them on the chart and takes hold of Emma's hands, taking note of the broken nails on her fingertips. These splintered edges are a harsh reminder that she woke up in a casket and tried frantically to claw her way out. Wren takes a sample from under the nails. She already knows that he would never allow his victims to come to a morgue with his DNA under their nails. But it is still a necessary part of the autopsy. Diligence pays off when you least expect it.

Wren moves on to the legs Emma's parents spoke of with pride to any doctors or nurses who would listen. They boasted about what a graceful runner their Emma was, her father's eyes filling with tears as he talked about how Emma accompanied him on evening runs as a child. His voice broke as he recounted how they challenged and motivated each other. It was clear he loved that their moments of evening bonding had turned into Emma's passion. When Wren broke the news that Emma was likely paralyzed from the waist down, it was devastating to them both. Wren had held it together in front of them, allowing them their right to grieve their daughter's immense loss, but that night she had finally crushed under its weight, letting the hot tears flow unimpeded in her dark living room.

Although they can no longer bound across pavement, Emma's legs are still strong. Wren can feel the defined quadriceps of a runner. She can see the long, lean muscles sculpted from years of training. Now wounds crisscross her skin, likely from running through a densely wooded area. She notices the lacerations on Emma's feet, like she traveled in harsh conditions without shoes on. She's seen this same pattern on multiple victims, herself included. She shakes the image from her mind.

"Where have you been?" Wren asks her, rubbing her thumb over the enormous scrape across the side of Emma's left foot. "Did he take you where he took me?"

She hears Leroux coming down the hallway now, his voice echoing across the corridor while he jokes with a couple of techs. He lets out an infectious laugh, and Wren's scrambled thoughts suddenly click into place. Leroux presses the button to activate the sliding door to the autopsy suite.

"All right, Muller, what's going on?" he asks as he steps through the doors. The look on his face is one of genuine concern, but Wren struggles to sort out which bomb to drop first. She turns to look at him, still holding the metal clipboard with Emma's external examination records.

"John, do you guys have any leads about where the killer pursued his victims?" she answers with a question of her own.

"You sure you're ready to get into it?"

She clears her throat and reaches out her hand to grip the cool metal table in front of her.

She nods. "You have no idea."

Leroux takes a seat on a rolling stool.

"Well, when you recorded the same types of wounds that one would get from running across a densely forested area in all our latest victims, we flagged it. He's clearly drawn to the chase, or rather, the hunt." He stops to take a breath and pushes on. "But what we can't figure out is *where* he's able to do this."

"A controlled environment," Wren finishes his thought. Leroux smiles.

"Exactly. There's not a chance in hell that this guy doesn't control the whole ordeal. It has to be a place where he can do what he wants without any real fear of them escaping. It's simulated risk."

"He has a house," she says without looking at Leroux, who nods along.

"For sure. He's got to have a pretty decent plot of undeveloped land because the injuries we are seeing aren't from running through a manicured backyard."

Leroux stands up, shoving his hands in his pockets as he often does when he's thinking through something. He begins to wander, pausing to look at anatomical models. Wren swallows hard.

"He inherited his parents' home," she says finally, almost in a whisper.

"Make sure you stretch next time you make a leap like that!" He chuckles, looking at her with a furrowed brow.

Wren bites at a piece of skin on her lip, taking a second to collect her thoughts enough to convey information coherently. After a beat, she turns to look at Leroux.

"I'm not plucking it out of the air, John. I know who is doing this."

Leroux's face twists into an incredulous smirk.

"What? Muller, is this what you were talking about on the phone?"

"Part of it. I know this man—he's capable, he is intelligent, and I imagine he's currently set up on his dead parents' land." She glances at Leroux, who looks as if she just told him she can fly. "It's Cal."

"Cal? Who the hell is Cal? Should I know that name? Cal who?" he stammers.

"John, do you remember the girl who survived the Bayou Butcher seven years ago?"

"Yeah, Emily something. I remember reading about her in my father's files. What does that have to do with this?"

Wren sucks in a breath, then meets his eyes. "It's Maloney. And it's me. I'm Emily Maloney."

It's like a ghost walked into the room. Leroux's face goes white as he struggles to find the correct words. He shifts his gaze down, clearly trying to connect it all in his head. He looks at her anew, trying to find confirmation in her eyes. Wren nods. He is silent, allowing her the space to continue when she's ready.

"Muller is my married name, as you know, and, well, I've just always kind of admired wrens. I thought it was a fitting name to hide behind."

He releases a gasp of air, almost smiling in disbelief.

"It suits you," he says, finally.

"Thanks, John." She softens and purses her lips, suddenly feeling weightless.

"My father worked that case," he says, trying to compose himself.

"He did. I remember him well, actually. He was the only one who listened to me and really believed me," she recounts and sits down on a stool, squeezing her eyes shut. "The officers who interviewed me thought I was on drugs or just confused from the trauma. I couldn't tell them where he had done it. I woke up out there practically blind, and I ran for miles without direction when I escaped. I couldn't even tell if I was in the same county. I was useless to their investigation, and they were angry."

Leroux's mind looks like it's racing. He opens his mouth to speak but stops himself.

Wren continues, "They said other witnesses described the Butcher as blond, and my description didn't match."

"I'm sorry, Muller. I don't know what to say."

"He must have dyed his hair brown when he met me. I told them that, and they ignored it!"

A sob escapes Wren, and she lurches forward and falls into Leroux's arms. He pulls her close as they both crumble to the ground together.

"I'm so sorry, Muller. I'm so sorry," he says over and over as they rock together on the cold floor.

"You don't have to be sorry, John," she responds, rubbing her eyes to collect herself. "I had moved past this. Had learned to live with it. But he's here again, Leroux. I know he is. The Bayou Butcher. Cal."

She meets his gaze with a stony calm before standing up and crossing the room. He lifts himself off the floor as she returns to his side with the bracelet. She drops it into his waiting palm, and he turns it over twice.

"E," he says, appraising the charm.

"For Emily," she adds. "That's my bracelet. He took it the night he abducted me. I found it with the rest of Emma's effects. He left it for me to find."

"Holy shit."

Leroux looks like he may fall right back to the ground, but he holds firm. He turns the bracelet over again in his palm, before pinching the bridge of his nose.

"Anyways, Cal had an elderly mother he spoke about sometimes when we were in class together. She was sickly and bedridden. I remember he said they had an old home and a lot of land. He loved that house. I bet that's where he's taking them. Where he took me."

He nods. His eyes move back and forth as he takes it all in.

"Philip Trudeau!" Wren blurts out suddenly and turns to look at Leroux. His face scrunches.

"Huh?"

She continues, "Philip Trudeau, the name on the library card. The one found in the book near one of the bodies."

"Yeah, I know, the guy from Massachusetts. I remember."

"I told you that name sounded so familiar. I was racking my brain that night. The name kept popping up, but I couldn't place it."

"Land the plane, Muller."

She waves his exasperation off and keeps going. "Philip Trudeau was Cal's childhood best friend. He moved to Massachusetts when they were young. He told me the story once after a lecture. I remember because it was such a weird thing to hold on to for so long. You talk to Philip Trudeau again, and I guarantee he'll confirm. That book, this bracelet. They were signs. He's been calling out to me the whole time."

"Don't forget he left your business card at a scene. This is starting to make so much more sense now."

"Call Philip Trudeau. Confirm he knows Cal," Wren directs. "Actually, John, maybe try the name Jeremy. The other victims, they called him Jeremy."

Leroux nods, taking this latest detail in stride after the conversation they've just had. "Are you okay?" Leroux asks plainly. "It's okay if you're not."

She smiles with her mouth, but it doesn't reach her eyes.

"I'm not. But I will be once this is finally over."

For a moment, they stay silent. It's a comfortable and safe silence.

"Hey, did you ever find out what the chapter from that book was about? The one you found at the Seven Sisters Swamp scene?" She doesn't look at him, instead keeping her gaze on Emma.

Leroux purses his lips, realizing the significance of this question now. "We did," he answers as she finally meets his gaze again.

"What was it?"

"The Most Dangerous Game." He answers directly, never letting his eyes stray from hers.

She smiles, shaking her head. "Cliché little bastard."

Leroux can't help but laugh lightly too. He clears his throat.

"We will sort this out, Wren," he says gently, using her first name pointedly. "I'll talk to Trudeau and see what I can find out about Cal-slash-Jeremy's current whereabouts."

He walks over to his suit coat and plucks it from the counter.

"In the meantime, if you need to put someone else on this case, do it. This could get really personal, really fast."

"Normally, I would fight you on this," she sighs, clicking the blade off the scalpel and flicking it into the red sharps container. "But I think you're right. I need to do what's best for Emma, and I'm not what's best for her right now."

Leroux crosses the room and squeezes her arm. Wren pulls a glove off her right hand with a snap. She grabs the phone from the wall and calls in another tech to finish Emma's autopsy.

CHAPTER 27

I<small>T'S RARE FOR</small> J<small>EREMY TO</small> feel out of control. He has patience. He has discipline. He has plans. But tonight, he has
none of that. Tonight, he just has anger. He's sitting in his car
outside of O'Grady's Pub, staring ahead at the only real path
left for him tonight. He can't get his last egregious miscalculation out of his head. Now he's buzzing, like a pressure cooker.
It was supposed to work. It was supposed to be theater, his vic-
tory lap. But the girl took his moment away from him, and it
hardly matters she succumbed to the hemlock. If he could, he
would go back in time to hack her head clean off and release
the rage inside him, but he can't.

And so, he hunts.

It's 1:30 a.m., and last call is near. This is the ideal time to
get someone to come home with him. It's late enough for even
the most cautious to cast their inhibitions to the wayside but
still early enough to catch people coherent and aware. He isn't

looking for a target practice dummy. He's looking for another rabbit that can run.

He quickly checks his reflection in the rearview mirror. His eyes are bloodshot, but in a darkened bar he knows they won't betray his state of mind. He carefully pushes a strand of hair that has fallen onto his forehead back into place and makes his way inside.

The bar is still packed. The air is thick with cheap perfume and even cheaper cologne. The lights give off a red tint that makes the one-room bar resemble the lower rings of hell. The remaining patrons are split into two camps. There are lone wolves who sit toward the ends of the bar with their shoulders hunched forward in a defensive lurch, inexplicably wanting to be left alone in this crowded room. He's not here for them. And there are the people who are still hopeful if not desperate for someone to notice them. Most of them don't even need compliments or even the veneer of decency. They just need the promise of pleasure to drown out their own self-loathing. Jeremy can work with that.

He doesn't bother with anyone standing around the edges of the space and instead makes a beeline to the bar. He slides into a seat and scans the room quickly. His eyes land on a woman sitting to his right, about three stools away. She looks to be in her mid- to late twenties, but worn, like she's seen all too much in her short time on this earth. Her brown hair has been straightened within an inch of its life and sits in a sharp spray just past her shoulders. He noticed her initially when she boorishly adjusted her blue strapless dress. She stuck her entire hand into the top of her dress to do so. He finds her utterly repugnant. Desperation rolls off her like cigarette smoke and mixes with the pompous delusion she wears all over her like drugstore perfume. And tonight, he's going to make her dreams come true.

He flags down the bartender with a finger in the air. She makes her way over to him slowly.

"What can I get ya?" she asks, wiping her hands on her pants.

"What is she drinking?"

The bartender looks where he is pointing and narrows her eyes, laughing. "Oh, that one is a Cosmo girl for sure." She looks back at him with a playful smirk, leaning on her elbow. "You want me to slip her a whiskey and see how it plays out?"

A smile hints slightly at the corners of his mouth. Bartenders can pick out a phony as well as he can, and for that they usually earn his respect.

He nods. "Give her another Cosmo and tell her it's from me, please." He slides her some cash to cover it, and she places her hand over it.

"You got it."

He watches her make the pink drink and pour it into a fresh glass. She slides it in front of Jeremy's mystery rabbit without spilling any contents over the rim—he's impressed. Rabbit looks startled but quickly transitions to satisfied. She feels emboldened now, pushing her hair back with a self-satisfied look on her pinched face. She glances up, after the bartender points her in his direction and casts a look his way under her eyelashes. She gives a flirty wave and beckons him closer.

Got her.

"I hope that wasn't too presumptuous of me," he says, sliding into the stool next to her, flashing his disarming smile.

She sucks in a breath. "I was hoping you would come over to talk to me."

She leans forward. He can plainly see her trying to subtly squeeze her arms to her sides to accentuate her cleavage. Her proximity makes him uncomfortable—she smells like tobacco and coffee, and it's nauseating as it swirls off her tongue in waves—but he soldiers on, concentrating on what's to come.

"Well, you're in luck then. What's your name, pretty girl?" He nearly chokes as he says this but keeps his voice steady.

She bites her lip.

"Tara," she answers in a breathy voice.

She draws out the long *a* in an obvious effort to appear seductive, and he almost pulls a muscle trying to stop his eyes from rolling. She smiles, and, unsurprisingly, doesn't ask for his name in return.

"Hi, Tara. I'm Jeremy."

"You don't look like a Jeremy," she coos and leans her chin into her palm, blinking her eyes rapidly. He forces a grin and takes a sip of his drink.

"Well, I doubt I act like one either," he replies, not even sure what it means but pleased that it's elicited a shrill giggle from his new friend.

This is too easy.

It's exactly what he is looking for tonight. No complications or overly intricate blueprints. He just needs release. The way he sees it, this is a return to the basics. All he has to do is get her in the car with him, and from there he'll be free to follow wherever his desires lead. He pauses to observe her as she sips her Cosmopolitan. She places it down and briefly wipes her nose with the side of her finger. She takes the same hand and runs it through her brown hair, flipping it to one side, and tilting her head back slightly in the process. As she does, he gets a glimpse at the tiny bit of dried blood that coats the inside of her nose.

Bingo.

"So, Tara, I've been watching you tonight." He smirks, seeing her light up already. "I mean, obviously, just the sight of you turns me on."

She's totally loving it and leans forward to allow him a better view down her dress.

"But I also know that you're the kind of woman who knows what she wants. You don't seem like the type to fall for a line of bullshit."

Her eyes travel down his body, and when they return to his face, she bites her lip, and replies, "Damn straight."

He recoils a bit but forces himself to move in closer. Just as he suspected—under her grown woman's exterior, she is just a horny teenage boy. He gets to the punch line, "I have some blow back at my place. Come with me."

He watches her eyes light up. She licks her lips in a way he's sure she thinks is alluring. "Let's go." She nods, leaning in too close.

He throws down some cash for the bartender's tip and stands, extending a hand to grasp hers as they walk toward the exit. The bar's smoky, hot air is replaced by the fresh evening breeze outside. He opens the passenger door of his car for her, and she slides in smoothly. As he walks to the driver's side, he mentally prepares himself and starts mulling over options. He should take her back to his place. But he doesn't want to wait for his release. Before sliding himself into the driver's seat, he nods to a man smoking a cigarette outside. He's frustrated, like he just got into an argument with someone, and gives Jeremy a perplexed look before flipping him off, stamping his cigarette out on the ground and going back inside the bar. People have a funny way of validating his disdain for them just when he needs it most.

They drive in comfortable silence for a bit. Every now and then, the woman breaks his meditative quiet with mindless bits of conversation. As the pair makes their way down the dark, tree-lined back roads of Orleans Parish, Jeremy decides where he is bringing her next. He turns onto a dirt road and distracts her with a bit of light conversation.

"What do you do for work?" he asks, preparing himself to feign interest in whatever menial title she's about to rattle off.

"I'm an attorney," she says, looking out the passenger window.

Her response is the first thing to shock him tonight. He stifles out an incredulous chuckle. "Really?" he asks, trying to keep his tone even. "A lawyer?"

She smirks, turning to face him with her glassy eyes.

"You sound surprised."

"I *am* surprised," he admits.

He shakes his head. She certainly doesn't come off as a lawyer. But he wonders what a lawyer would look like in the last hours of the night at a dive bar. This woman just occasionally cut a line with her bar membership card before snorting another hole into her brain.

She laughs lightly, then shakes her head too.

"Well, I have the title, but I just lost the first job I got out of law school," she admits, stopping short of an explanation and flicking her shame-filled eyes down to her hands.

He can tell she wants to talk about it. She is looking for a companion to unload on, but it won't be him. No, she won't find any empathy or thoughtful advice over here. He has infiltrated her broken world for sport, and he's only interested in his own games tonight. She looks over at him but quickly turns back to the window once she sees that he isn't going to press for more information.

"So where exactly do you live?" She shifts uneasily in her seat, feeling the weight of her spontaneous decision. "Should I be nervous that you're turning into the woods right now?"

She clears her throat nervously but turns it into a forced chuckle. He smiles, keeping his eyes on the road in front of him.

"No need to be nervous, esquire. I live a bit off the beaten path."

A smile tugs at the corner of her lips, but her nervous energy lingers.

"You live down here?"

"Not down this particular road, but close enough."

He keeps his eyes focused in front of him. The road before them is dark, unlit, and bumpy. A swamp emerges on their left, and menacing cypress trees knit together like a screen to their right.

"So why are we going down this way if you don't live here?" she asks, posturing bravado. She clutches her seat belt like it's a weapon.

He pulls into a dirt patch near the swamp and cuts the engine. Finally, he smiles over at her.

"The air is so nice tonight. I thought we could go for a walk," he reassures.

"It's, like, pitch-black," she protests but can't help but follow like a lamb to slaughter.

He smiles, walking toward her. He can see her stiffen as he strides into her space. He leans forward, and she sucks in a quick breath just as he reaches into the open car window to snatch a flashlight. He wiggles it in front of her face and then clicks it on. The inorganic sound cuts through the silence.

"Not anymore," he says with a wink, taking her hand in his.

Somewhere in her brain, she can feel herself in danger. Her body tenses, and her pupils dilate. Together they stroll into the deep darkness stretched out in front of them. The only light is the moon, which is close to full. Its light is bright white and gives the whole area a slight glow. She is gripping his hand. She clings to it as a child would cling to their parent's. He squeezes it in a simulated show of comfort. They walk in silence for a few minutes, both examining the terrain around them, though for completely different reasons.

"It's actually kind of pretty out here. It's still really creepy but pretty."

She startles at a twig snapping in the distance, and her body instinctively leans closer to his out of fear. He can't help but smile at the irony. He is far and away the greatest threat to her safety in this bayou.

"Yeah, but all things worth considering are an amalgamation of scary and beautiful. How boring it is to fit into only one category."

"I bet you assume I don't know what *amalgamation* means, huh?" She pauses and looks up at him, smirking in a way that makes her look more attractive than she did in the badly lit bar.

He grins back, waiting for her to continue walking. She shakes her head as they make their way toward a wooden bench by the water. It's crudely cut and clearly handmade, but somehow also inviting, making the filthy swamp look peaceful. They sit side by side and look out at the moon's reflection on the surface of the murky water.

"I passed the bar exam, you know. Believe it or not, cleavage doesn't correlate with intelligence."

She is smiling good-naturedly. He doesn't respond right away, taking a moment to feign scratching his leg to feel for the holster holding his hunting knife firmly in place near his ankle.

"Guilty." He straightens up, casting his eyes on her. "You are a good example of the dangers of judging a book by its cover."

She laughs softly, playfully bumping her shoulder into his. "That's a strange compliment, but I'll take it."

"How generous of you."

"How could I really be mad at that face?" she admits, and places a hand on his left cheek, turning his face slightly to meet hers. She closes her eyes and begins to move forward, initiating a kiss. He hesitates only slightly before moving to close the distance, almost touching her lips with his own. Once he can feel her breath meet his, he speaks softly.

"You should run."

The words slither out of his mouth. Her breath hitches, and she smiles nervously. She keeps her face close to his but pulls back just slightly to look into his eyes.

"What?"

"You heard me correctly."

Her smile drops quickly. She pulls back and lets out a puff of incredulous breath.

"That's not funny."

"It's not supposed to be."

He can almost feel his eyes darken as he bends down to slip the knife from its place on his ankle. He holds it up in front of him, inspecting it and admiring the moonlight bouncing off the blade. She is paralyzed where she sits, her eyes flicking from him to the weapon. He can see regret flash across her face like a movie trailer.

"Now, run!" He yells the last word at her, never once turning to meet her gaze as he does.

Out of his periphery, he can see her take off into the darkness as a choked sob escapes her mouth. He stands as well, giving her a moment before walking in her direction. There's nowhere for her to go. He brought her to a dead-end trail, lined with swamps and completely surrounded by barbed-wire fencing. The parks department's efforts to keep the alligators out has now locked her in with the real predator. Her options are to face him or swim.

He knows this place well. His father used to take him here often to hunt feral hogs when he was young. He was taught patience on those evenings that they spent together, waiting for hogs in this secluded playground. Somehow, they managed to carry out their illicit excursions without incident from local law enforcement. It's a pleasant memory, watching over the swamp as night fell.

Hunting at night is a lesson in fear. It teaches you to control your instincts and accept the unfamiliar sounds that slither out from hidden places once the sun goes down. Night dwellers know that the silence is a myth. It is always loudest at night. He's able to distinguish between each of the hundreds of different sounds that make up this nightly chatter. A real hunter can tune it all out to listen for its chosen prey. Tonight, his keen ears tell him he's on the right path. Of course, he has no interest in hunting hogs now. He puts into practice the countless skills he honed out here with his father in a different way today. He's since found a far more exciting prey.

Through the cacophony, he hears a twig snap to his right. He can tell that she has stopped running. He would be able to hear her running. He walks softly, allowing the earth to absorb every step before placing the other down. He smiles as he strides.

"Calm down, Tara! Did you know that the meat actually tastes worse when the animal displays extreme fear before slaughter? Something about the lactic acid breakdown."

He hears her stifle a sob. Her breathing has become loud enough to make out clearly over the din.

"Oh, Tara. I don't want to eat you!" He laughs now, stepping over a fallen branch. "It's interesting though, right? Do you think we've even tasted meat at its finest? After all, how could any animal be completely serene before its death? You're enjoying my little fun facts, aren't you, Tara?" He yells into the darkness when he reaches her name.

She's running again. He can hear her take off through the brush. He hears her stumbling footsteps and ragged breath move farther away from him. Her panic is detectable even in the murky darkness that surrounds them both. He breaks into a sprint too. He lets the branches whack his face as he sails through the familiar terrain and enjoys the unbridled rush of an old-fashioned chase.

Ahead of him, Tara might as well be blind. He can hear her stop and start several times as she attempts to navigate the pitch black that spills out in front of her. Endless minute noises give away her location. Then, suddenly, the commotion stops. He stops with it. He stands in the middle of the trees and listens. She's hiding, he assumes. She doesn't know yet that he knows these woods well. He knows where a scared little piggy would take cover. He breathes in the crisp night air and tilts his head back to look up at the sky. It is vast and clear, framed by the cypress tree branches that reach out to cradle it.

He pulls the night-vision glasses from his pocket and allows his eyes to adjust. He also learned from his father to use thermal imaging equipment to stalk alpha predators that similarly reveled in the night once the last bit of light slid beneath the horizon. His world is green and focused now. A wall of trees stretches out in front of him, punctuated by small swampy areas and natural rock formations.

"Tara!" he calls out, shattering the silence. "I can see everything, Tara. If you try to run again, I will shoot you."

He's lying. There is no gun in these woods. He says this to increase her panic. He's accelerating her fear response, strong-arming her amygdala into sounding the alarm that something threatening is nearby. He has to wait only a few seconds before her hypothalamus will trigger her sympathetic nervous system into giving away her hiding spot. Her heart is beating faster now, lungs opening to suck in as much oxygen as they can, increasing her alertness but creating much more noise as her breathing quickens. He focuses on that breathing now. He begins to follow it. He imagines her crouching in the muddy forest, trying to ignore the creatures that make their way onto her bare legs uninvited. It's got to be torture for a girl like her. She's been ripped completely out of her element and fully immersed in his.

He gazes at his surroundings through his glasses. Everything in his view is cast in a sickly green hue, but to Tara it's as dark as the inside of an executioner's hood. He moves, called by her breathing as it becomes choked and frantic. She can hear him coming toward her, but she can't see him, no matter how hard she tries to focus her eyes. She can feel the fear take over her body like it's replaced the blood in her veins.

He hears her stumbling through the branches and underbrush and pauses momentarily to listen. The bayou will do its best to help him, but it will try even harder to trap her. She runs toward the dirt path they came down earlier, splashing water as her feet pound into the earth below. She has no idea that she's running farther into his cage.

He runs toward her now, bursting from the tree cover into the open expanse of the dirt path. She hears him and turns to digest what little the moonlight reveals. Her face is lit with terror. Jeremy smiles widely, stalking toward her with the knife unsheathed. And Tara, now exposed, screams as she breaks into a clumsy run. It's like she's running through sand. He seizes the opportunity to gather two tennis-ball-sized rocks from the ground.

"Duck!" he yells out, startling her enough to stop and cover her head instinctively.

He throws one of the rocks with as much force as he can muster. It connects with the back of her leg, making her crumble to her knees in an unnatural way. She wails in pain and shock, frantically reaching for the source of the blow. He throws the second rock. It ricochets off her skull with a sickening crack. She falls to the ground, now clutching her head.

"Stop! Please stop!" she cries out.

But he doesn't. He slowly walks toward her broken body in the middle of the path. As he crouches down next to her, she swats at him aimlessly. He catches her hand by the wrist, holding it up to the blade in his. He feels her pulse racing under his fingers and then drags the blade across her palm. She screams, trying to pull her hand back with everything she has left. As her screams turn to sobs, he smiles. He's in control again.

"Is someone out there?" A man's voice echoes out through the night, snapping Jeremy back to attention. Flashlights appear at the far end of the dirt path.

"Are you hurt?" a second voice calls out.

Jeremy can see the shapes of the two men entering the path. He claps his hand over Tara's mouth before she can cry out for help, but panic starts to creep into his veins. They heard Tara. He didn't scout out this location ahead of time tonight. He had acted on impulse, and he didn't consider the hunters sitting in the very same ground blind locations that he had once occupied with his father.

"We aren't here to hurt you. We'll get you help," the first man continues gently, swinging the beam of his flashlight toward them.

Tara's eyes are wide, silently screaming out to these men, but they can't see her. Not yet.

A pang of frustration rings through Jeremy's chest as he weighs his options. In the end, there is only one path forward.

Still muffling Tara's mouth with one hand, he lifts her chin to look at him. He takes one final second to relish in the moment when their eyes lock before hearing her would-be rescuers rush closer. He quickly brings the bowie knife across her neck, slicing deeply from ear to ear. As soon as the blade releases from her flesh, he drops her to the ground and takes off running. She sputters and gurgles behind him, and the men rush toward the sound. Deep, disjoined breaths heave from her tattered larynx as they arrive at her side. The wound spans the entire length of her neck, and it's deep. They bark orders at each other, one of them calling for an ambulance and the other frantically trying to slow the bleeding. It won't do much good though. Jeremy is sure he cut her carotid artery. She will be gone within minutes as her body forcibly pumps its own life force from her wound into the dirt.

He runs, not stopping as the chaos unfolds behind him, propelling himself farther and farther away with each bound. He dives into his car and flicks off the headlights before peeling away in a cloud of gravel and dust. He uses the night-vision goggles to guide him as he makes his way back to the main road. No other cars follow. The men are too busy trying to save a woman seconds from death.

Jeremy just drives, flicking the headlights back on and removing his eyewear when he's put enough space between them. He opens the glove compartment where his phone sits and presses play on a random playlist. "Pretty When You Cry" by VAST plays loudly, and he takes in a deep, calming breath. Today was a bad day. In his brain, he knows he should have just stayed home. He should have dealt with the repercussions of his last miscalculation before piling another mess on top of it.

He's sure Tara will die. But it's the sloppy execution that bothers him. He dove into the water without even checking the depth. He was foolish and impetuous. He acted on animal impulses and ignored his prized brain. Without a thought, he swerves the car toward the side of a dark road, throwing it into park as dust swells around the headlights. He pounds his fist against the steering wheel, wails on the vinyl surface like it holds a treasure locked inside. When his hand throbs and his breath is heavy, he sits back in his seat and screams. All his stress and frustration, all his dissatisfaction and hunger erupt in a primal scream on the side of a dark, dirt road deep in the

Louisiana bayou. Tears roll down his face, and he lets them cool his burning, dirt-covered cheeks.

His chest heaves as he throws the car back in drive and barrels toward his home. He turns the music up loud, hoping it will drown out his thoughts. The barrage of sound only fuels the anger he can no longer control. As he speeds down the road ahead, he knows his days in this place are numbered.

CHAPTER 28

Leroux's phone buzzes from his coat pocket, and he takes the moment to answer it.

"Leroux," he answers and taps his phone to put the call on speaker.

"It's Will. Can you hear me?"

"Yeah, what do you need?"

"We have another victim."

Will drops the statement like a brick. Leroux winces, and Wren's heart sinks along with his. She rubs her hands down her face.

"Oh my god," she whispers.

"Where?"

"She was found in a hunting area off Bayou Tortue Road. But Leroux, she's alive and conscious."

Leroux's eyes go wild.

"She can talk?" he asks incredulously.

"Not quite. She's alive, but she can't talk."

"What the fuck does that mean?"

"Just meet me at University Medical Center. I'll give you the entire story once you're here."

The line goes dead.

"I'm coming," Wren states. She turns and starts washing her hands in the sink.

Leroux opens his mouth to speak but closes it again, watching her.

"Spare me your concern. I appreciate it, but I need to hear what this woman has to say myself. I'm part of this."

She dries her hands and locks her eyes with his. He lets the silence hang between them for a beat longer before gesturing his head toward the imposing metal door.

"Let's go."

Will is standing outside, talking to a doctor when they arrive at University Medical Center. Leroux strides up to them, not bothering with introductions.

"So, what's the deal?" he asks, interrupting the conversation mid-sentence.

"Dr. Gibbons, this is Detective John Leroux and Dr. Wren Muller."

Dr. Gibbons extends a hand to Wren first. She shakes it and smiles as best she can.

"We've met. Nice to see you again, Dr. Gibbons."

"Always a pleasure, Dr. Muller. And nice to meet you, detective."

"Yeah, same here, so what's going on?" Leroux steam-rollers, still firmly grasping the doctor's hand.

The doctor nods, placing a hand gently on his arm, and starts, "Now that you are all here, we can discuss this together inside."

He gestures to the building behind him, and the four of them enter together. He leads them into a small room with some chairs and a large table. It's meant to be a more private space for families to wait and receive updates away from the main waiting area. Will and Wren sit across from Dr. Gibbons, but Leroux remains standing, rubbing his hands together.

"Spill," he commands once the door closes.

Will opens a notebook in front of him, leaning back and reading it off like a grocery list.

"Tara Kelley. White, female, twenty-nine years old; found by two night hunters in Elmwood Park off Bayou Tortue Road. The guys reported hearing some screaming and commotion. When they ran up to her, she was holding her throat, which had been slashed deeply only moments before."

Leroux stops him, leaning over the table.

"Was it him?" he asks angrily.

"Possible. Though it's shocking that he would get this sloppy now. Doesn't really fit his MO. But I suppose it happens to all these jackasses the longer they go."

Dr. Gibbons stays quiet as Leroux and his deputy volley their questions and answers back and forth. His lips are pulled into a tight line as he waits to speak.

Leroux shakes his head, slapping a hand on the table.

"Dammit! But she'll be okay, right?" Leroux asks, moving his eyes from Will to the doctor now.

Wren can already tell what the answer is, but she stays quiet, trying to disengage from the situation and remain professional.

Dr. Gibbons clears his throat, and answers, "The short answer is yes, she's stable. The wound was substantial, spanning from ear to ear. Her attacker likely intended to sever the carotid artery, but, instead, perhaps in a moment of haste, just nicked it. She still suffered immense blood loss, but thanks to the men who found her, the bleed was abated to a degree that we could work with. She came out of surgery about an hour ago."

Dr. Gibbons's eyes reflect Leroux's exhaustion.

"When can I speak to her?" Leroux asks pointedly.

"Well, she can't vocalize right now. Her attacker did manage to sever one of her laryngeal nerves and damage her vocal cords. She won't be able to speak while she heals from surgery." Dr. Gibbon's stops for a moment to pull a piece of paper from the file in front of him, sliding it across the table to Will and Leroux. "The paramedics who brought her in said she was frantically trying to tell them something, so they gave her this piece of paper to write it down."

The torn notebook page is smeared with dark blood. In blue pen, barely legible enough to make out, it reads "Jeremy."

Wren feels her breathing get faster and shallow. Shock radiates through her system like electricity. Even though she knew already where this path would lead, she still can't fully believe that this man has been walking around Louisiana all this time. That is, until she had it spelled out for her in ink by a bleeding woman.

"Should I know a Jeremy?" Will questions, struggling to catch up.

Dr. Gibbons clears his throat again. "The police who arrived on scene collected a few items from the immediate area around her body, including a receipt for where she was earlier in the evening. I'll have someone bring them to you before you leave. Good luck, gentlemen. Dr. Muller." He nods as he walks to the doorway.

"Thank you, Dr. Gibbons," Leroux almost yells.

"Leroux, who is Jeremy? What's happening here?" Will tries again.

"I'll fill you in later," he says quietly, glancing at Wren.

Will is about to protest when someone knocks gently on the door. Leroux crosses the room to open it, and standing outside is a young orderly holding a hospital bag in front of him.

"Detective Leroux?" he asks.

Leroux holds out his identification and badge and takes the bag from his hands. He immediately looks for the receipt and finds it in another small bag. It's from O'Grady's Pub with a time stamp of 1:22 a.m. The credit card number is attached to the name Tara Kelley and shows she had at least two Cosmopolitans and one side of fries that evening. He looks at his watch.

Will motions for the receipt, and Leroux hands it over after dialing the number of the bar. He gets an answering machine message telling him no one will be there until noon.

"This is Detective John Leroux from the New Orleans Police Department. Please call me back as soon as this message is received. Thanks."

"No one there?" Will asks.

"I'm waiting for Cormier to send me the owner's information now. We can just go talk to him directly. I want to find out if anyone else saw Tara with our guy last night."

Will lets out a puff of air. "Muller, you coming along?"

Wren looks at Leroux, silently questioning.

"If you feel up for it," Leroux concedes. His phone chimes, and he looks down at the address and phone number displayed across his screen. "Let's go pay a visit to Ray Singer."

Together they leave the room the same way they came in. The sun is shining brightly, and a couple of media vans are parked out front. The latest victim is big news, and, apparently, it's traveled fast. Wren takes in the scene before sitting down in the passenger's seat of Leroux's car. Jeremy is still out there, doing the same things he did to her all those years ago. But this time, she's going to stop him for good.

CHAPTER 29

JEREMY WAKES UP FROM A fitful sleep. It's Sunday, the day the world typically reserves for rest, but it just won't come. The previous evening still weighs heavily on him. He feels uncertain. It's a feeling he hasn't had to confront in a long time, and recently it's near constant. He flicks on the television, imagining that by now Tara will be splashed all over the news. He should feel triumphant, but the degree of sloppiness takes away from his pride. As soon as the news report begins, he feels his heart stop.

"The victim, twenty-nine-year-old Tara Kelley, was rushed to University Medical Center, where she remains in critical condition," the news anchor reads like a footnote, like it isn't the single most crushing blow Jeremy has ever felt.

"Could we have a potential serial killer on our hands?" the anchor asks, almost salivating at the chance to report on another death.

It's disgusting, really, the way these folks go from six to midnight for a murder. Of course, it's human nature to be curious, to explore, to prod through the darker parts of our psyches. Really, who is he to judge? But something rubs him the wrong way about these reports read through strangled smiles. The reporter on his screen says the victim was able to give some pertinent information to the police. He freezes, waiting for more, but she stops there, saying updates would follow as they became available.

He swallows hard. Another fuckup.

Emma was dead. The hemlock had secured his secrets behind its impenetrable wall. But Tara is different. Picking her was impulsive, and it was reckless. In his haste to feel something, he hadn't brought her to the safety of his own home or even bothered to scout the area ahead of time. He just assumed that Elmwood Park was abandoned because it had been when he had hunted there with his father as a child.

"How did she survive?" he asks himself out loud.

He knows he dragged his blade across the correct spots. It's something he could never mess up. He feels the failure of just missing the mark again. Missing a major artery is just another reminder of the grave error that led to Emily's escape all those years ago. Both should have been left rotting in the daytime heat, undiscovered until it was all too late.

"Fuck!" he yells, throwing his spoon in the sink with a crash.

He leans back into the counter and looks around his home. He can't think of a way out of this, and the feeling is unfamiliar. He could run. He could move on to another place, where his movements won't be so magnified. It's the only choice left really, but first he wants to bring Louisiana to its knees.

He strides down the rickety staircase, dragging his fingertips along the exposed rock on the walls. The ancient basement has been updated with a cement floor for functionality, but the bones of an old dirt cellar remain. His father never bothered with making the cellar useful. They used it for storage, but he did all his work outside. When his mother died, Jeremy turned it into his workshop. It was a decent space that had been neglected for too long.

He knows this may be the last time he feels these walls, the last time he listens to the stairs creak and groan beneath his feet. He takes his time. He collects souvenirs with every blink. He never fixed that one light bulb in the corner. It's been flickering for months. At first, he had just kept forgetting to change it, no doubt distracted by the pleasures awaiting his arrival downstairs. Eventually he had come to appreciate the ghostly glow of the dying bulb. It made the basement look scarier, like a mad scientist's lab or Leatherface's workshop. But he won't be needing the grim ambiance any longer. As he reaches the bottom step, he grabs a fresh light bulb from the box on the shelf to his right. He reaches up easily to unscrew the blinking bulb in the back corner and replaces it with the new one.

Fixed.

The steady light changes things. Without the strobing effect, everything softens. He lets his gaze wander around, wishing he had more time.

It won't be long before they arrive to tear this place apart. Soon, this will all be reduced to evidence bags and caution tape. Somehow, his current situation is made worse by the knowledge that it was a noncompliant woman who toppled his house of cards.

If this is how his story is going to unfold, he is going to take control of everything he can. He unlocks the pristine deep freezer situated neatly against the wall and enters numbers into its keypad lock. The latch clicks loudly, cutting through the soft hum of the air conditioner. He runs his hand over the top of the lid. It's cool to the touch as he drums his fingers along the smooth surface. When he opens it, the vacuum seal gasps. It reminds him of lungs deprived of air for almost too long. A blast of cold air hits him in a wave as he gazes down at her. She's freezer burned. Her skin is like ice, smooth and cold. Dried blood still cakes her cheek. After weeks in the freezer, it has dried and now stains her skin. It looks beautiful in a strange way, like a macabre rouge.

If he turned her over, he'd be able to touch the neatly bandaged wound in her lumbar region. He got it right that time. With this experiment, he had successfully severed the spinal cord at the C6 vertebra. Immediately, his captive lost movement in her legs, trunk, and arms. That's what was supposed to happen seven years ago, but he has since learned from his botched attempt, perfected it.

An incapacitated victim is easier to work with, but less of a challenge; perfect for a test of scientific prowess rather than athletic endurance. He always wanted to attempt a lobotomy, ever since those early days at the library. She had bled more than he anticipated when he inserted the ice pick into her orbital socket. His initial attempt at the prefrontal lobotomy didn't go quite as planned. But the father of the ice pick lobotomy had had failures too. Admittedly, he hadn't anticipated how difficult it would be to place the ice pick in the correct position. Even when he knew he had made a mistake, he still proceeded to the next step of stirring it around, and that's what really ended things for her. She had shuddered and convulsed. Her eyes bulged, and she tensed so hard that he was sure she would break. Her pain was evident on her face. He can still see her muscles reflexively tightened around her neck and jaw. She would have gritted her teeth down to dust if he hadn't placed the gag in her mouth. Blood dribbled from her nose like a leaky jug of milk and pooled below.

It's like lipstick now.

He touches the dehydrated skin with his fingers and relishes in the feeling. The bright blood had glistened on her lips and teeth at the time, shiny and inviting. Now it looked like the cracked surface of the driest desert. The ball is still there between her teeth, hardened from the cold. At the time, he thought it was just a bit of practice, but now her suffering will have a greater purpose.

He unplugs the freezer, propping the lid open. When they come, they will smell her first. He unlocks a closet to reveal his most heavy-duty tools and weapons. His preference has always been to hunt up close. Even when he was younger, he enjoyed sticking a pig with a sharp knife more than shooting it from afar. Sometimes a situation requires distance though.

If he is going to hunt big game, it's time to bring out the big guns.

He grabs his TenPoint crossbow and a quiver full of titanium mechanical broadhead arrows. When deployed, two blades shoot out from the sides of each arrow, resulting in a two-inch wound on the target. Maximum damage without added bulk. He'll be able to move easily and quickly, vital to his plans. After all, this is the first time his prey will be able to shoot back.

CHAPTER 30

Pulling up to Ray Singer's address, Leroux sees Will leaning against his parked car. He parks behind him in front of the home and gets out.

"I'll stick behind here for a little," Wren says from the open window. "I just need a minute to process alone."

Leroux nods. "Okay, we won't be long. Don't touch my radio."

He throws her the keys, and she gives him a small smile as she starts up the engine.

"John, why must you always make me wait for you?" Will waves his arm dramatically, and Leroux rolls his eyes.

"Get it together, Broussard."

He tucks in his shirt and starts toward the front door. They walk up the steps and ring the doorbell. A disheveled-looking middle-aged man answers the door. Even from the safe distance of her place in the car, Wren can hear everything with total clarity.

"Can I help you?" he asks, opening the door and leaning out.

Will speaks first, showing an ID as he does. "New Orleans Police Department. I'm Detective Broussard, and this is Detective Leroux. Are you Ray Singer?"

Ray looks stressed.

"Yes. What is this about?"

Will continues, "We are investigating a near-fatal attack that occurred in the area last night. The victim was last seen at your bar."

"Jesus. Is it that woman from the news?" he asks, his eyes widening.

Leroux nods. "We need to speak with the bartenders and any waitstaff that were working last night. Can you provide us with those names and their contact information?"

Ray leans against the doorframe, running a hand through his messy brown hair.

"Wait, the Butcher was in my bar? Is that what you are telling me? Holy shit."

Leroux holds up a hand and interrupts, "We just need the waitstaff and bartenders to tell us if they saw anything out of the ordinary last night."

"Of course, right. I'm heading in now to open up, and some of the staff from last night will be there too. You're welcome to follow me there."

"Great, we'll do that."

Will gives Ray a curt nod, and the three men head back to their vehicles.

Leroux's phone rings.

"Leroux," he answers, pausing at the car door before ducking back into the driver's seat.

"Hey. We have someone here who thinks he may have some information about the Elmwood Park victim. He was at the bar last night."

"I'm coming in right now." He hangs up, looking up at Will. "Possible witness at the station. I have to head in now. Can you take care of this?"

"Ten-four," he responds jokingly.

"Call the station. They can give you the rest of the details."

"Yeah, go on! Let me know what ends up coming of it."

Leroux turns his attention to Wren. He keeps his gaze soft, like she's a piece of glass he doesn't want to break.

"Take me home, John," Wren says quietly and looks out the window, suddenly feeling the weight of the day crush in on her.

"Of course." Leroux nods, starting off in that direction.

The air between them is heavy. Neither of them is willing to discuss any of the information they've learned today. Wren puts her hand out the window and lets it undulate in the warm air, and it pounds against her as they drive.

CHAPTER 31

JEREMY WATCHES HER.

Standing in the sea of deep black that floods the tree line on the edge of her property, he tracks her movement through the windows of her home. He knows her well enough to anticipate her turning on every light in the room even at this late hour. Emily wasn't scared of much, but she was always wary of what awaited her in the darkness. Even as he stands in the pitch dark, he is cognizant of this fact and makes sure to keep himself obscured behind branches and stands halfway behind a massive tree. He knows her routine now. He knows where she sits to decompress at the end of a long day. He has watched her for a long time.

He waits.

He stands perfectly still and listens to the chorus of invisible, nocturnal insects that hum all around him.

He thinks about how interesting it is that in the dead of night, humans seem biologically programmed to detect every single noise that seems out of place, even among the deafening sounds the surrounding environment makes on its own. If he did so much as cough, it would be noticed. Yet the forest can scream all night with no consequence.

Until tonight, he has just observed her and left little clues from afar.

He watches her double-check the locks on all of the windows and doors. She never goes to sleep without making sure she is locked in safely for the night.

She is thorough, and she is smart, but during his surveillance, he has discovered that there is still one way to penetrate her fortress that she consistently fails to secure. Her basement is unfinished and, thus, entirely neglected by her. She and her husband took precautions to have an impressive lock installed on the bulkhead door that leads from the yard into the basement but have not yet installed one on the door that leads from the basement into the house. After all, as long as no one can enter the basement, there is no need to worry about anyone coming up from down there.

Jeremy noticed only three windows leading into the basement. Two of which are too small for anyone larger than a small toddler to fit through. The third window is the one he is interested in breaching tonight. This third window is bigger and opens conventionally. It is equipped with a lock, but one that is clearly broken. When he first came upon it during one of his quiet night visits, he immediately became suspicious. It just doesn't seem to be in Emily's nature to leave a window unlocked. It's shockingly irresponsible to leave a broken lock untouched. This house is lucky to have remained unbreached up to this point.

When he attempted to open it, he confirmed that it was merely painted shut. This little detail made him assume that the basement was designated as her husband's responsibility and Emily probably just trusted that he had sufficiently seen to the securing of the space. Stupidly, he must have assumed that a broken lock is not worth replacing if the window itself has been painted shut since long before they moved in.

Emily looks out the kitchen window. There is a puzzled expression stretched across her face. She appears to be deep in thought. Before she walks outside his view, there is a moment in which it almost looks like she might see him. He feels her meet his eyes for just a second. Of course, she didn't, not really. The light behind her will ensure that.

He watches the light flick off but doesn't move. He will stay obscured for a bit longer, so he can be sure that he has given enough time for Emily and her husband to fall deeply asleep. He doesn't mind waiting. One of the qualities that has served him best is his extraordinary patience, something that he's been neglecting recently and to his own detriment. He won't make that mistake tonight. He'll check himself out and allow the time to carry him through to safety. Two and a half hours in a blink. A gasp of air. An instant if he wants it to be.

He makes his way through the heavy darkness to the un-secured basement window. The ancient paint seal is the only thing keeping him from crossing into Emily's space. The only way to get through it is with a blade. Jeremy is prepared. He takes the knife from his boot and lightly saws along the sill. The aging, yellowed paint cracks like an eggshell beneath the recently sharpened blade. Decades of poisonous lead flecks float into the air and flutter to the grass beneath his feet. He wonders when this window was last opened and who painted over it to begin with. The type of person who painted it shut is the kind of person who cuts corners. Why would anyone choose to underperform? Society has always bred such mediocrity.

Jeremy is glad to see the end of this window's reign of deceitful surety. Negligence eventually leads to vulnerability, and no one is more vulnerable than someone who is asleep in their bed. Once the seal has been sliced, he removes a screwdriver from his pocket and wedges it in between the sash and the sill. Using the handle of his knife, he hammers until the window lifts with a crack. Dust and paint swirl into the darkness as the window takes its first breath of Louisiana air. He steps through the new opening and directly onto a dusty worktable that houses a leaf blower along with a vast array of miscellaneous lawn tools. After steadying himself on the unstable surface, he shimmies onto the floor and waits for his eyes to adjust to the darkness that reaches out from every corner.

The stairs are old, and they groan quietly as Jeremy ascends them to the first floor. Pushing open the door to the kitchen, he notices one of the lights has been left on. It illuminates the corner where the trash can sits, and he wonders whether there has ever been a time when someone desperately needed a trash can in the dark.

He moves slowly, anticipating the creaky floors that always come with old houses. Leaving the kitchen, he enters the room where he watches Emily sit most nights. He runs his gloved fingers along the antique dresser that stretches across the wall to the right. It's old and looks like it belongs in this home. There are myriad quirky odds and ends prominently displayed across its top like trophies. He pulls open a drawer to find it filled with a mixture of assorted mints. The surprising contents forces a quick, unexpected chuckle from him, and he shakes his head as he closes it again.

He notices pieces of her scattered on every visible surface. It would be clear to anyone who enters her home that Emily discards items as she moves through the house—a ring on this table, a bracelet on that counter. She leaves a breadcrumb trail of her night. None of the pieces he sees is special. None of them is the item he needs. He presses on, knowing that what he's looking for will call out to him when he comes across it.

He stands at the bottom of the staircase and stares up into the darkness, allowing his eyes to adjust again to the blackness that leaks out from the upstairs hallway. He steps onto the first stair and presses his shoulder into the wall as he climbs. There is no way that this staircase is a silent one. He places his feet carefully, making sure to let each step land like choreography. Wooden stairs have a habit of expanding and contracting with changes in the atmosphere. With this in mind, he knows that placing his foot in the middle of the stair will almost certainly elicit sound. With the movement of a cat, he stays on the edge closest to the wall. As he makes his way up, he passes photos encased within mismatched frames lining the stairway and is careful not to hit them as he passes by. When he reaches the last step, he pauses. The doorway to his left is closed, and a fan quietly hums from the other side of the door. That's where Emily is sleeping. It took a few nights to ascertain this particular bit of knowledge, but his vigilance paid off when she forgot to pull down the shade of her bedroom one night. He observed her wake up sometime around three a.m. and make her way to the bathroom, which sits to the right of the stairs. When she came back into the bedroom, she pulled the shade after taking a quick look out the window.

He takes a breath in and slowly shuffles to the door, pressing his hands against the wooden frame. He listens to the soft, rhythmic breathing that is barely audible over the fan and turns his back on the door to slide down to a seated position on the floor. He leans his back against the door and tilts his head to one side, so his right ear is flush against it as well. He sits. He listens.

Another hour goes by while he sits outside of their bedroom. He feels powerful. He imagines Emily and her husband waking briefly to roll over or look at the clock, oblivious to the fact that someone is right outside of their bedroom door. He likes the feeling of violating their sense of security. He likes knowing that they feel false safety in their vulnerable state. That he could kill them both with one slice of his blade. Of course, he doesn't intend to kill them tonight, though he wants to. That is not how he's operating this time around. No more unplanned releases.

Tonight, he is here for something other than blood. He slowly rises to his feet and pauses to steady his breathing. He isn't nervous. It is the genuine feeling of excitement quickening his breath. He places his hand on the doorknob and turns it slowly. The door opens without a sound. Emily and her husband lie motionless in the bed across from the entrance and don't stir even slightly as he enters the room. He walks softly, allowing his eyes to readjust to the different shades of darkness in this space. Making his way to the left side of the bed, he crouches next to his Emily and looks over at the contents of her bedside table.

Sitting next to a dog-eared paperback is a ring. It is big, expensive-looking, and covered in diamonds. She never wears it in public. He has never seen something that ostentatious on her delicate fingers. Anyone would have been able to surmise that it's special to her. He is sure this is the one she mentioned to him before in passing conversation between lectures all those years ago. It belonged to her grandmother. He picks up the ring and can see a light film of dust that surrounds the clean circle where it once rested. It sits on this table as a permanent fixture. A comfort item, and exactly what he is looking for. He slips it onto his pinkie. But before he rises from his crouched position, he takes a final look at Emily. She's facing away from him with one arm on top of the blanket, her auburn hair spilling onto the pillow from an untidy bun piled on the top of her head. She's clutching a handful of the same blanket in her right fist. He can smell her. The smell is clean. Not flowery or specific, but distinctly clean.

He could end it now. He could reach out and snap her neck before she ever realized there was someone next to her. He could plunge the screwdriver into her temple or slit her throat with his blade. He could snuff out her life in an instant. The feeling is overwhelming for a moment, and it almost overrides his plans completely.

But just as quickly as it came, the feeling leaves. Jeremy knows that isn't the way their story ends. Emily won't gasp her last breath without knowing who took it from her. He stands again and lightly crosses to the doorway on the other side of the room. Facing the bedroom, he turns the knob and holds it in position while he silently closes the door. Once safely out of the room, he slowly releases the knob back into its original position and makes his way to the top of the stairs for a slow descent to the main floor.

He exits the house the same way he entered, and as he creaks the basement window closed, he takes a sharp breath of night air into his lungs. Touching his thumb to the ring on his pinkie finger, he walks the tree line once again and disappears into black.

CHAPTER 32

WREN LOOKS AT HER PHONE. The message notifications and news alerts pile up mockingly on her home screen. There's a missed call from Leroux, and a follow-up text at the top of the barrage urging her to call him back. Richard squeezes her shoulder in a small show of comfort. He sits down across from her at the table in their kitchen. His face is kind. She feels empathy for him and his position in this. It's an impossible situation to react to, and somehow he is doing it perfectly.

"You don't have to be part of this, Wren," he says after a moment or two of shared silence.

She looks up, eyes tired and mind blurry. The hits haven't stopped coming over the last few weeks. After Leroux dropped her off, she tried desperately to take her mind off the case, but more details kept bubbling to the surface. She couldn't get the image of the other victims out of her head, especially poor Emma on the cold, sterile table. And then it hit her. The hemlock. Such a strange and unique murder weapon. In fact, it's so rare that she's only ever seen it once before in her career.

"I know. And thank you for saying that, but I have to tell the others what I know," she replies, playing with her rings on her fingers. "I've been working this case for weeks. And I've been living in the Butcher's shadow for years. No matter what the conclusion is, I have to help."

Richard nods, leaning his elbows on the table.

"I trust you. Just take it at your own pace, okay? Call John back when you're ready."

"I suppose there is no time like the present," she replies and stands up, already beginning to pace as the phone rings in her ear.

"Muller, hey," Leroux answers after two rings.

"Hey. Before you start, there's something else I need to tell you. Remember that case I had a few years back? An older woman brought into the ER by her adult son. She had a history of depression, a few past suicide attempts, and he said that he thought she might have ingested something in another attempt that evening. She was reportedly convulsing significantly and having trouble breathing." Wren pauses, waiting to hear if Leroux remembers the details of the case. "She ended up with me not long after being brought into the hospital because of what we later found to be hemlock mixed in with her nightly glass of red wine."

"Hemlock? People use that stuff?" Leroux asks. Wren can almost see him shaking his head, desperately trying to understand the connection here.

She continues, "Poor thing was almost shattered to pieces from the muscle convulsions. She barely made it ten minutes in the ER before heading my way. It is a horrific death, and for that reason, not an obvious mechanism for suicide. But there was no indication of external foul play."

"I actually do remember this. Wow. What was that? Two, three years ago? We all questioned it, sure, but like you said, there was nothing concrete to go off."

"I have only come across one other hemlock death in all my years as a medical examiner. The woman we found at the cemetery."

"You think they are connected."

"It's him, John. I know it."

"What was the woman's name in the other hemlock case?"

"Mona. I remember she looked like a Mona. I already looked it up in the system. Her full name is Mona Louise Rose. Next of kin listed as Jeremy Calvin Rose."

Leroux sighs on the other end of the phone. Wren takes a deep breath and squeezes her eyes shut as she paces.

"Well that name isn't new. We spoke to Philip Trudeau. You were right, he's the same guy you thought he was, and Jeremy Rose is a name he floated to us."

Wren suddenly feels light-headed. It's undoubtedly the result of the information flooding her already overloaded brain with no sleep and a steady diet of vending machine fare over the past few days.

Leroux powers through the silence. "I had someone who was at the bar last night come forward. He saw a guy leave with the victim. His description wasn't all that helpful. Just mentioned that the suspect had smiled at him, and it was memorable somehow."

Wren isn't surprised that a witness mentioned Cal's smile specifically. His smile *was* memorable, mainly because it was slightly crooked. Something about it was charming and gave him a strange air of ease when he flashed it.

"Yeah, I can see someone remembering that about him," she says quietly, eyeing Richard at the table, who is listening with concern.

Leroux continues, "I'll follow up with him and see if we can get a positive ID for Jeremy Rose."

He clears his throat, his voice hoarse.

"I'll put together an affidavit to bring before a judge after we get an address for the Rose property. We have to try to get to him as soon as possible because he will likely try to run. The news is running a bunch of shit, and he no doubt knows he fucked up now."

"I'm coming down there. I want to go with you once you get the warrants."

Leroux scoffs. "Wren, no. This is too much. You have done enough already. Without you, I wouldn't have as much on this creep as I do. You kicked this all into gear. You deserve to take a step back."

"I appreciate that, John. I do. But I'm coming. How are you so sure there aren't going to be more bodies on his property? We still have a few open missing persons cases, and I wouldn't be shocked to find them rotting out there in his swamp. A medical examiner should be there."

"Wren . . ."

She interrupts, "And besides, if he tries to run or is hiding, seeing me may draw him out. After all, he made a lot of effort to get my attention. Why would he hide from me now?"

Leroux sighs. "I'm not using you as bait, Wren."

"I know. I just need to be there. Let me be there," she pleads.

There is silence again on the other line. After a whispered curse, he concedes.

"You're a big girl. I can't stop you from going when you have a valid reason to. Meet me at the station. Broussard just got here, so I'm going for the warrants now."

"Okay, I'll see you soon."

She hangs up the phone and looks back at Richard. His kind face is twisted with concern.

"I don't want you to go," he says forcefully.

She knows his fears are valid. If the situation were reversed, she wouldn't want him running into this situation either.

"Richard, I know this is scary," she begins, crossing the kitchen to sit next to him in a chair.

"It's not scary, Wren. It's horrifying. And so dangerous! This guy tried to kill you. He tried to end your life, and he waited years to come out of hiding just to lure you to him," he exclaims, breathless. "Now you want to walk right into his house? That's insane. It's insane, and I can't let you do it!" Richard's voice breaks. He claps a hand over his mouth and shakes his head. "I'm sorry. I won't."

"I know. I know. But I'll be surrounded by law enforcement. John and Will, and a bunch of other armed officers, will be there. You can trust them to keep me safe, and I won't do anything to put myself in danger."

"More danger, you mean."

"I will come home to you. I promise. I just. I have to close this out. I have to see him taken away in handcuffs, or I'll never sleep again. Please try to understand this."

She is on the verge of tears, the physical exhaustion and emotional toll starting to wear down at the strong walls she works so hard to keep standing. Richard looks down, collecting himself for a second before looking back up again. His eyes blink rapidly, holding in his own tears. His eyes are red-rimmed and fearful. He grabs her hands.

"Come home to me," he pleads.

She squeezes his hands back, leaning her head so her forehead is against his.

"I promise."

CHAPTER 33

JEREMY SPINS THE ANTIQUE RING between his fingers.

As he walks through his home, he slows his breath and attempts to cultivate some calm. This beautiful, decrepit farmhouse has been an extension of him throughout his entire life. He grew up here, learned lessons here, and now he hunts here.

He chuckles to himself, dropping the ring into his pocket as he runs his hand down an intricately carved doorframe. For a second, he can't believe everything is about to change, that the carefully constructed structure he exists within will be forced to shift. He can feel something ignite inside of himself. Like a power surge, he instinctively punches the same wooden frame he had been caressing. He sees red, first from his newly cracked and bleeding knuckles. They throb as the broken skin pulls apart with each flex of his fingers. He lazily smears it on the white doorframe, dragging his fingertips in it as blood droplets crash to the floor below him. He blinks several times, but the red remains. It's everywhere. His greatest failure will force him from this sanctuary, and he's never felt anger like this.

She'll pay.

He stalks into the living room at the front of the house and feels positively intoxicated with rage. He finds an antique crystal vase in his hand, turns it over, and feels like if he squeezed it hard enough, it would turn to dust in his palm. The blood from his knuckles smudges onto the green-tinted glass, and before it can slip through his grip he throws it against the wall in front of him, letting a guttural growl escape his lips as he does. It shatters into a beautiful, dangerous rain. A mosaic of glass bounces to the ground around his feet.

Jeremy pauses, looking down at the shards of glass as the light dances around, reflecting off his chaos and creating a prism effect. He stands there, panting. Rarely has he known such animalistic rage. He takes a long breath in, using his unbloodied hand to carefully move a strand of blond hair from his forehead and tuck it back into place. He makes his way to the kitchen and carefully turns his hand over to examine his tattered knuckles. He creaks on the sink and begins to wash away the evidence of his lonely outburst. As the blood changes from red to pink, mixing with the water swirling into the steel sink below, he gazes out the window into the stretch of bayou that seems to touch the other side of the Earth. After what could be a minute or an hour, he dries his hands, wrapping the three damaged knuckles in medical tape and flexing his fingers for comfort.

He walks again, floating through the rooms in this house and taking snapshots to commit to his memory. He will use these memories to tether him to who he is. He doesn't have plans to die today. He finds himself back in the living room, where the evidence of his anger still remains. He doesn't clean it up, preferring to leave it there as a message and a threat. He hopes they wonder whose blood this is, even just for a moment. He hopes the crunch of shattered glass disrupts their neatly planned raid.

Reaching into his pocket, he fingers the ring once more. His gaze shifts to the coffee table in the center of the room. Its position is center stage, and he places the ring on its surface in a spot that's impossible to miss. It's stationed alone on the surface like a single boat lost as sea. He smiles, stepping back to see the effect for himself.

Welcome back, Emily.

CHAPTER 34

WREN SITS IN THE BACK of the room now. The police station is a chaotic scene, with officers being given orders in every direction. Leroux and Will entered the building thirty minutes earlier with a search and arrest warrant in hand. They got a positive identification from their previous witness and the bartender who served Tara her drinks.

"All right, does everyone know what they should be doing and where they should be?" the lieutenant booms over the circus around them.

Leroux sits in the chair next to Wren, leaning forward with his arms resting on his thighs.

"You got your kit?" he asks abruptly.

As if shaken from a deep sleep, she jumps.

"Yeah. Yeah, I have my kit in the car. Why?"

"Because you're coming with me. If there are bodies to process, we can call in more techs with the vans, but I want you in our car." Before she can protest, he shakes his head. "I promised Richard I wouldn't take your shit. This is nonnegotiable."

"Can't argue with that!" she says, putting her hands up in surrender.

Leroux stands, extending a hand to help her up as well.

"That's the attitude I want you to have even after all this is over."

She pushes him with whatever strength she has left, and he feigns a stumble.

"Don't count on it, John."

The back seat of the car is not Wren's favorite place to be. It's always led to almost instantaneous motion sickness since she was a child. Today is no different.

"I can't tell if I want to throw up because of your driving or because we are about to ambush the guy who tried to hunt me in his backyard," she says as she opens the window. She rolls her eyes, letting the breeze calm her stomach a bit. "You guys can laugh. Please laugh."

Leroux and Will both release a chuckle.

"Jesus, I never saw this being my job," Will says, wiping his eye.

Leroux looks confused. "No? You never saw yourself catching a prolific serial killer? Isn't that kind of the point?"

"Well, yeah, of course. But it's never been quite this dramatic, you know?"

"Yeah, I guess you're right. This whole thing has been very *True Detective*."

Wren chuckles now.

"You think I went into the death industry for this kind of drama? I mean, yeah, I'm a cliché for spending my life speaking for the victims of brutal killers after almost becoming one myself," Wren jokes, and rubs her hand across her face. "But I chose the morgue for a reason. It's quiet and controlled."

They sit together in comfortable silence, riding along the isolated back roads of Jefferson Parish, heading toward the Montz area. Leroux was able to find the address of the Rose property easily enough, and now they're on their way to it. The home sits on a large swath of land outside of the well-trodden paths frequented by outdoor adventurers year-round. As the tree line becomes thicker and the roads bumpier, she can tell they are approaching their destination. She can feel the sickness rise again in her throat as she grips her medical bag and rubs her rings with her thumbs.

When they pull into the long, winding driveway leading up to 35 Evangeline Road, the air seems to thicken. All three of them silently take in the isolated surroundings, following the two other police vehicles ahead of them. Without warning, the home comes into view. It's like a shot of adrenaline to the chest. Wren's heart beats fast and hard. Her breaths become quick and shallow, and her face heats up. A panic attack is nearing, but she manages to use the breathing techniques she learned from therapy sessions long past to slow it down. She takes in the air through her nose and slowly releases it through her mouth.

The home has been taken care of as well as it could be in the middle of swampland. It's old, but the yard is well maintained and clean, with a new-looking Nissan Altima parked in the driveway. A stretch of bayou and cypress trees sprays out from the back of the property as far as the eye can see. Docks and boardwalks sparsely dot the landscape, but most of it is untouched and natural. It's both beautiful and horrifying, the perfect hunting ground for a monster.

Leroux turns his body to face her in the back seat, a look of concern across his face.

"We've got a lot of bayou to cover. You still okay, Muller?" he asks.

She nods, knowing she doesn't look okay, and confirms, "I'm fine."

He waits for a second to look for hesitation in her face.

"Okay, we're going to have a team go in and clear the place first. If he's in there, they will detain him. They're going to make sure we don't walk into any kind of ambush, especially with you," Leroux briefs and takes in a sharp breath. "We aren't letting you out of our sight."

"I understand. I trust you," she says gratefully.

He nods and turns to Will, who is watching the first team of officers surround the house. They knock on the front door and wait. The anticipation is already strangling Wren. Nothing happens. After a couple of attempts, they kick open the door. The team rushes in from all sides, entering the home in a frenzy.

Wren closes her eyes tightly. Everything suddenly sounds muffled and warped like noise-canceling headphones have been placed on her head. She waits for gunfire or an explosion. She waits for something terrible to happen, but nothing does. It's just muffled footsteps and controlled shouts from inside confirming the rooms are clear.

A young officer dressed in tactical gear steps out onto the front porch. He waves his arm at Leroux and Will and shouts, "He's not in there! All clear!"

They nod in response and open the car doors to exit. Leroux lets Wren out from the back, and she steps into the oppressively hot air.

"It smells like death," she says as soon as the air hits her nose.

Leroux scrunches his nose up instinctively.

"No kidding. It definitely smells bad."

Wren shakes her head, and corrects, "No, it actually smells like death. There is a corpse around here somewhere."

She scans the area now. The three of them make their way to the front porch, stepping up onto the peeling paint that has barely survived the harsh Louisiana weather over the decades. They step into the front hallway, and the smell intensifies. She imagines he can't smell it as acutely anymore after so much time entrenched in it. Will and Leroux stay on either side of her as they walk into the living room. The dated furniture feels like stepping back into the 1940s. There is a green velvet chaise longue stationed in front of a beautiful set of windows. The lamps are intricately designed and cast a calming light over the room. Art pieces cover the walls, various paintings from different eras and styles. It's part museum and part bordello. If she weren't so terrified, she'd almost find it charming.

Then she spots it.

Sitting in the middle of the coffee table, on a mirrored platter, is her grandmother's ring. She walks to it, crouching down to view it at eye level. She doesn't wear it because it's too small for her but always keeps it at her bedside table. It is a comforting thing to fall asleep next to. But because she's barely slept in her own bed for days and when she did was too engrossed in work, she hadn't noticed that it was missing.

"John." Her voice breaks, and she grips the sides of the coffee table. He rushes to her side, placing a hand on her back.

"Muller, what's the matter? Do you need to leave?" He frantically searches her face and then moves his eyes to the ring in front of her. "What's going on?"

She suddenly feels like she is in danger. She scans around her, waiting for him to rush out. He doesn't.

"This ring. It's from my bedside table," she says flatly, not taking her eyes off it.

His jaw drops, and he waves over a photographer to take a picture of it.

"Muller, do you mean this used to be on your bedside table when you were last involved with him?"

She shakes her head slowly, finally bringing her eyes to meet his. "No. I mean, this is from my current bedside table. From my current home. This was taken from my bedside sometime in the last week." She stands quickly, taking a moment to steady herself as Leroux rises with her. "He came into my house, John."

She chokes back a sob, feeling her body lurch at the thought. She can feel herself spiraling.

"Wren. I don't know what to say. I truly don't know what to say," Leroux says, biting at his lip anxiously.

"It's okay. We'll deal with this later. I can deal with it later. Let's keep going," she says, hardening her resolve.

"Blood here," Leroux points to the doorframe, which is streaked in fresh blood. Droplets have rained down on the floor below it. Wren's eyes move to the shattered green glass to her left, and she notices pieces have fresh blood smeared on them as well.

"Maybe someone cut themselves on this broken glass," she says flatly.

"Take some samples," Leroux instructs another officer and waves Wren over to the next room.

They make their way into the kitchen next. It's spotless and bright. A coffee mug sits on the counter, half drunk. A shiver runs down her spine. As they move into the dining room, another antique, bordello-themed time warp, an officer from the second floor yells down to them about a box with some of the possible victim's clothing in it.

"Mind running up there?" Leroux gestures to the photographer, who hurries up the creaky stairs to the second floor.

"There is definitely something dead outside, but judging by the strong smell in here, there has to be someone in here as well."

"We were told about something in the basement." Will shifts on his heels. "They said they thought it was just the smell permeating the house from outside, but then they spotted the open fridge."

"The fridge?" Leroux raises his eyebrows.

"Shall we?" Will steps aside to let them go in front of him.

Wren nods and follows Leroux down the basement stairway. The odor chokes them. It's got a different layer than the smell upstairs or outside. This is thick enough to feel like wet sand as they push through it down the stairs.

As they turn the corner at the bottom, Wren doesn't feel any familiarity here. She's never been in this basement, but it is exactly how she pictured it. It's clean, sterile, and organized.

Near the back of the basement, close to the wall, is a row of chairs. They are sturdy, with thick arms. They remind her of courthouse furniture. As Wren moves closer to them, she sees that they have been bolted to the floor, with a layer of cement keeping them in place. The arms are encircled with leather straps and solid chains, rusted, and coated with thick, red-brown blood. The seats of these chairs all have blood smeared and pooled on them, and more of it has dripped down their legs and onto the light-gray cement below.

"I'm guessing these weren't for Bible study," Leroux quips and crouches next to her, using a gloved hand to shake the leg of one chair, which doesn't budge. "Make sure we get someone down here to take samples of this."

The air is thick; Leroux uses the sleeve of his shirt to protect, almost smother, himself against the pungent stench of decaying flesh. Wren has moved on to the white freezer in the corner. The lid is open, and the plug has been tossed to the ground. The smell becomes fleshier. The layers of stink burst like grenades with each step closer. She hovers close to the freezer, willing herself to look. She isn't scared of the dead. She's afraid of what they have to say.

"Muller, what's in there?" Leroux asks, still standing over by the chairs.

She sees her now. She's young, her blond hair darkened with blood and various other bodily fluids that have escaped in this unhallowed resting place. Her red, lifeless eyes were once green or blue. But now they are cloudy and bloodshot. Her cheeks are swollen, and Wren can see where the blood poured from her eyes, nose, and mouth after some kind of traumatic injury.

"What did he do to you?" she asks out loud. She reaches her gloved hand out to touch her, but she stops herself.

"Well, at least we know where the smell is coming from." Leroux appears next to her, gesturing for another officer to come take over. "Let's go upstairs and maybe get some air for a second."

Wren spins around to face him, breaking from her trance for a moment. "What? No. This is exactly why I came here. I'm the medical examiner. There are bodies to be processed."

"Of course, Muller, but this is a lot. It's okay if you just need to get some fresh air for a second. No one would fault you," Leroux says and lightly bumps his shoulder into hers in a show of comfort.

"I'm okay. This is my job. I just need to go get my kit. I left it upstairs," she replies sternly, and walks over to the stairs, sparing a glance at the chairs once again.

Her heart races in her chest, and the smell of rotting flesh and men's cologne begins to mix into a sickening cocktail. Her head is woozy, but she shakes it off. She hears Leroux and Will follow close behind her and can hear their hushed conversation as they climb to the ground-floor kitchen.

"Don't leave her side while you are up there," Leroux says quietly to Will, almost too softly for Wren to hear.

"Of course," Will answers gruffly.

As she grabs her kit on the table, she centers herself a little bit. As she turns to descend the stairs once again, an older officer emerges from the hallway.

"Do you guys hear music?" he asks.

Wren strains to listen amid all the movement in the house. Will and Leroux also perk up. She does hear something off in the distance. It's faint and sounds like it's coming from outside.

Leroux waves them on. "Come on. It's outside. We have officers in the back, checking it out now."

The three of them make their way outside, and the music becomes clearer. The ocean of trees before them remains still but not silent. It is still a bit muffled, but it is unmistakably "Black Magic" by Badwoods cutting through the organic orchestra of the bayou. The soundtrack is sickeningly upbeat, and the dissonance is haunting. Wren takes a shaky breath in, trying to rid herself of the anxiety that threatens to consume her.

"This has Cal written all over it," she states, remembering the feeling of being suffocated by music in her most terrified moments as Emily.

"Was he a theater kid?" Leroux shoots her a subtle smirk as he looks over his shoulder.

She is thankful for the lightness he brings this moment, and replies, "No, though I imagine he's making up for that now."

They walk down the rickety back porch steps and step onto wooden planks that lead to a thickly forested area. Cypress trees hug one another from every angle, and the sun can't penetrate the blanket they form over this area. This is where he took his victims. This is where they cut the skin on their legs and feet while trying to run away from him. The feeling in this place is dark and ominous, saturated with the evil that has touched it for so long.

They enter the backyard together, with one officer behind them and one in front. Leroux and Will both have their guns drawn. As they stride forward together, the music gets louder, competing with the cicadas that are humming loudly from the trees. The smell of decay becomes almost too much to take as they go deeper into this hunting ground. When they reach the water, she spots its epicenter.

"We have the source of the smell," she hisses, pointing to the dark, crumpled body lying beside the swampy water.

The three of them move as a unit, and the smell of decay becomes otherworldly. The body is decomposing rapidly, thanks to the weather and the insects, but Wren identifies the victim as male. There is an apparent wound to the side of his temple that looks like it could be from a gunshot. Wren snaps a quick photo on her phone, and she grabs tweezers from her kit to go to work. She dislodges the bullet from its entry wound, holding it up at eye level.

"Good thing you're here, Muller. You were right," Leroux shakes his head, covering his mouth and nose with a gloved hand.

She smirks, dropping the bullet into a baggy and placing it back into the medical bag. As she snaps the latch shut, Leroux arches his back and lets out a howl like an injured animal. He slumps forward, then falls onto his side. He grasps his left leg. Wren's eyes fixate on the hunting arrow sticking out of his calf. It's metal and long. The wound it creates is larger than she expected. Wren leans over to start tending to him.

"Officer down!" Will yells.

As soon as he does, another shot is fired in their direction. This one meets its mark in another officer's back. He falls forward, and Wren can't help but scream. Leroux is groaning in agony, grasping at his leg and scanning the trees manically. Will stands over Leroux and Wren now. No one can determine where the shots came from in the chaos, and now they feel like sitting ducks.

A twig snaps.

"Emily."

The voice is calm, and it's familiar. Wren looks up from Leroux's wound and sees him. He steps out from beside an ancient tree, holding the crossbow in his hands. He levels it directly at her. His long hair has fallen onto his forehead like it used to when she last saw him. He's wearing a black T-shirt with dark jeans and black combat-style boots. He looks calm and satisfied. He takes a moment to size her up. Under his gaze, she immediately feels transported back to that night seven years ago. She feels the same urgency and the same rage. He has those same dead eyes, and over the years that have passed, they have become even darker.

For a second, she just stares back at Cal, at Jeremy, or whoever he is today. She knows what he is capable of. She slides Leroux's gun out of his grip and stands, training it on Cal. He keeps the bow aimed at her, and his crooked smile spreads slowly across his face. He drops the bow to his side.

"Shoot him!" Leroux bellows from below her.

She hesitates, momentarily frozen in place, unable to move her finger to squeeze the trigger. And suddenly there is a pop. She watches as he stumbles back, dropping the crossbow and holding his chest. He drops to his knees, and rolls his body into some underbrush nearby, immediately disappearing in the thick growth. The sun struggles to reach through the canopy of trees. Darkness lurks all around even in the daylight. Wren is still paralyzed with fear, holding the gun still aimed at the blank space where he stood only moments earlier. She looks to her right where Will stands protectively, lowering the gun he just fired. A sharp puff of air escapes her lungs.

Officers run toward the underbrush with Will close on their heels.

"Muller, stay with Leroux!" he yells over his shoulder.

All she can do is nod, still staring at the spot where Cal just stared her down. She can hear breaking branches and incoherent orders, but it's like her head is underwater. She forces herself to stay on alert, and a sound cuts through the air. It makes her heart race and a cold sweat form along her forehead. Two gunshots, about ten seconds apart, cause the birds to scatter and screech overhead. She stares wide-eyed for a moment. Every cicada, bird, toad, and leaf works in tandem to scream her into the present. She listens.

"Dr. Muller."

A young officer emerges from the trees, causing Wren to jump and clutch the gun tighter in her hand. He sees her fear and holds his hands up, speaking softly. "Sorry for the alarm. Broussard is with the suspect. We just need to confirm that he's deceased."

Wren lowers Leroux's gun, breathing in another gulp of hot air and nodding. She looks down at Leroux.

"Are you okay here?"

"Do I have a choice?" he jokes and winces with the effort, grabbing his leg. "Be careful, Muller."

"I'm okay. Call the medics down for him, please," she directs the young officer.

He steps closer to them, already grabbing his radio on his shoulder and asking for medics to come down the path. Wren sighs, wiping the sweat from her forehead and walking toward the trees. She can hear the officers speaking close by as she maneuvers her way through thick roots of ancient cypress trees. Spanish moss tickles her face. She sees broken branches and heavy footprints in the dirt. Everything moves and breathes. The scene is heavy and alive.

"Muller." Will startles her as she approaches him. "He put one in his own mouth."

He says the words bluntly, and she swallows to process this information as fast as she can.

"I'll confirm," she answers. "And thank you."

He squeezes her hand as he passes her by. "Don't mention it."

She lets go of his hand and strides toward Cal's body. He's on his back now, blood spattered across his face and chest. His eyes are open, staring up at her from the wet ground that surrounds him. Always so clean and together, he finally looks like the monster he was inside.

She snaps a glove onto her hand and leans down to check his pulse. There is nothing.

"He's expired," she says coldly.

She pulls out her cell phone and dials the office, letting the deputy examiners and techs know to come over. As she turns to face the officers behind her, something catches her eye. Something about the face looking up at her seems off. She uses her gloved hand to wipe away the blood from his face, slightly turning it to look at her straight on. As she looks into this man's green eyes, she can feel her heart stop. Her hands fumble to lift the black T-shirt over his abdomen, searching for the wound from Will's earlier shot, and instead finds smooth, unviolated flesh.

"This isn't him," she says disbelievingly. She falls into a seated position and scrambles backward on the ground to put distance between herself and this stranger. For the first time, the dead have her scared.

"Of course it's him!" Will rushes forward to grab her shoulders. "Muller, what do you mean?"

She shakes her head, feeling panic rush up inside of her, and shouts, "No! It's not! This isn't him, Will!"

"You recognized him back there. I saw it. You both recognized each other."

"I did. We did. It was him out there. But not here, not now," she explains and takes a deep breath. "There is no bullet wound where you shot him."

He moves his mouth to speak but nothing comes out. His gaze rests on the lifeless body nearby, and it's clear he is trying to find the logic here.

"That's impossible. I shot him in the chest."

"If this was a self-inflicted gunshot wound, where is the gun? He didn't shoot himself. He was shot by the guy who set him up for us to find."

Will's eyes dart back and forth between her own and the body. He looks up and sharply points a finger at an officer standing to their right.

"Search this place inside and out. Find him. Now."

The officers scatter in different directions.

He looks back at Wren and calls for an officer, who rushes to their side. "Bring Dr. Muller back to Leroux and make sure they both get out of here safely with the medics."

Wren opens her mouth to protest, but Will cuts her off again.

"Your job is done. Go with Leroux to the hospital."

Wren stands and squeezes his arm before turning to walk back through the thick green vegetation with the officer protecting her in tow. As she makes her way up the path toward the ambulance parked on the lawn, she waves to the paramedic.

"I'm coming," she says.

The medic nods, opening the doors to reveal Leroux on a gurney. He is sitting up and gives her a look of relief.

"Is it over?" he asks.

She shakes her head, taking a seat next to him on the small bench. The doors close with a bang, and the engine roars to life.

"No," she responds softly.

Leroux tries to catch her eyes, but she can't bring them to focus.

She lifts them to meet his gaze.

"He got away, John."

CHAPTER 35

Jeremy emerges from the swamp outside his property and stops to catch his breath. The bulletproof vest under his T-shirt rubs against his sweat-covered skin. He never wants to wear one of these again. It's binding and suffocating, but he is thankful it worked when he needed it to. Sucking in the humid air around him, he fingers the welt on his chest that is beginning to swell and turn red.

Better than a bullet wound.

He pushes forward through the thick swampland stretching out before him. The warm water soaks into his pant legs, leaving a layer of slime behind. He can feel the mud pulling at his boots with its deep suction, trying to free them from his feet. He waves away a cloud of mosquitoes, and they spread out momentarily only to reconverge around him with increased fervor, ready to brand him with a million itchy wounds for his insolence.

It won't be long before Wren discovers that the body he left behind is not him. Once she does, he has no doubt that she will put it all together quickly. She's just as smart as he remembers, and she's motivated by a deep anger. It radiated from her eyes when they met his own. Like the mosquitoes who attack him ruthlessly now, Wren was hungry for his blood before this, and would be insatiable now. But he'd won this battle, and soon he'd win the war.

She couldn't shoot him. He watched her finger hover over the trigger but never squeeze. He wonders if that would change now. He wonders if she would hesitate again, given another chance. Unfortunately for Wren, she won't get that chance. He will be hundreds of miles from this place soon enough. As he shifts the backpack on his shoulder, he pushes his way through the trees that grab and scratch at him. There isn't a path through here, but he still knows his way well enough. His father once brought him here to try his hand at hunting gators. Of course, they never caught one.

He's keenly aware of the monsters who share this space with him. In the dark, their eyes gleam like they do in nightmares. They move slickly through the muck with tails capable of incapacitating a man faster than any weapon. They are the true bayou butchers, ruthless and bloodthirsty. And tonight, he'll be one of them.

The sun sets low under the horizon, and the night sounds rise in sync as he walks toward the road stretched out ahead.

ACKNOWLEDGMENTS

To my John, thank you for always being supportive and encouraging even when I was sure this writing thing was not going to work out. Thank you for watching the babies while I sat outside and pounded away at the keyboard, drinking hundreds of coffees whenever a quick burst of inspiration came. Thank you for giving me the confidence to start this book at the first sentence. I love and appreciate you endlessly. You are a true gift. I promise never to hunt you in the Louisiana bayou.

To Karen, thank you for being the mother-in-law that no one believes can exist. You are selfless and always willing to send me away to write while you do something fun with the kids. You are appreciated more than you can know, and this wouldn't have been possible to finish without you.

Mom and Dad, I know I dedicated this to you already, but since you gave me life, it bears repeating. Thank you for giving me the tools, confidence, and love to write this nightmare. As a kid, you held my hand through night terrors, and now I am handing one right back to you. I swear it's a compliment and a show of love. Trust me here. I adore you both.

Ash. You are my best friend, my sister, my niece, and my business partner. You look great in every hat that I make you wear, and you are a vital part of me finishing this book. Thank you for always reading it out loud to me, so I could hear it from a different voice, and thank you for allowing me to horrify you daily.

To my siblings. Amy, you are my big sister and one of my best friends. You were the only one who was allowed to wash my hair when I was little, and while I can't say that's still true (I wash my own hair now), I appreciate looking up at the birdies to this day because of you. Thank you for providing a smiley-fries-and-ranch-dressing kind of love.

Jp, my big brother and also my twin in another dimension. We look alike, we think alike, and we would both probably mess with the Lament Configuration and unleash a hellscape of Cenobites unto this world, but we would high-five regardless. Thank you for encouraging me and creating with me.

Thank you to Dr. Stone. You gave me a chance to enter the world I had always wanted to step into, and I am forever grateful for what you have taught me. This book was born from the autopsy suite, and you are the reason I am able to experience it.

To my squad: Seth, Andy, Marissa, you rock in a way I can't describe. That's a big deal because in the immortal words of Josie "Grossy" Geller, "Words are my life!" Thank you for being people I can count on, and for making me feel like this was possible.

To my literary agent, Sabrina. Sabrina, we are one now. You are stuck with me for life. Thank you for dealing with my madness, my neurosis, and my constant need to be in control and informed about every single detail of everything that ever occurred during the creation of this story. You made me a better writer, and I am glad to have gained you as a friend in the process.

To my amazing editor, Sareena. I feel like the universe put us together. The second we met, you got me, you got my story, and you helped me turn it into what it was always meant to be. I appreciate you so much. You made this book happen, and you made it the best it could be. Even Jeremy would be impressed by you, and that's both impressive and terrifying. I'm so glad you took a chance on the weird little world I created.

To Zando, thank you for seeing this book like I see it. Thank you for making my dream of becoming an author come true.

Thank you to Stephen King, Patricia Cornwell, R. L. Stine, Christopher Pike, Edward Gorey, Alvin Schwartz, and Stephen Gammell. You helped me accept the dark, spooky, scary, and odd parts of myself that I tried to fight for so long. Thank you for inspiring weirdos everywhere to create with their strangeness.

To New Orleans. I hope the spirit of your city is felt in this book. Thank you for giving me such an inspiring place to inhabit in my head.

ABOUT THE AUTHOR

ALAINA URQUHART is the science-loving co-host of the chart-topping show *Morbid: A True Crime Podcast.* As an autopsy technician by trade, she offers a unique perspective from deep inside the morgue. Alaina hails from Boston, where she lives with her wonderful husband, John, their three amazing daughters, and a ghost puggle named Bailey. She is about 75 percent coffee, and truly believes she and Agent Clarice Starling could be friends.

Before writing her first psychological horror novel, she received degrees in criminal justice, psychology, and biology. When she isn't hosting *Morbid*, she hosts the Parcast original show *Crime Countdown*, and a horror movie podcast called *Scream!* Her days are usually spent either recording or eviscerating. The way she sees it, when she hangs up her microphone for the day, it's time to let the dead speak.